HARSH CONSEQUENCES

A Novel by

John W. Gemmer

CCB Publishing
British Columbia, Canada

Harsh Consequences: A Novel

Copyright ©2016 by John W. Gemmer
ISBN-13 978-1-77143-290-0
First Edition

Library and Archives Canada Cataloguing in Publication
Gemmer, John W., 1948-, author
Harsh consequences : a novel / by John W. Gemmer -- First edition.
Issued in print and electronic formats.
ISBN 978-1-77143-289-4 (hbk.).--ISBN 978-1-77143-290-0 (pbk.).--
ISBN 978-1-77143-291-7 (pdf)
Additional cataloguing data available from Library and Archives Canada

Cover artwork: Caribbean stormy day © lunamarina | CanStockPhoto.com

Disclaimer: This novel is a work of fiction. Names, characters, businesses, and incidents are either a product of the author's imagination or are used fictitiously. Any resemblance to actual persons, living or dead, is entirely coincidental.

Extreme care has been taken by the author to ensure that all information presented in this book is accurate and up to date at the time of publishing. Neither the author nor the publisher can be held responsible for any errors or omissions. Additionally, neither is any liability assumed for damages resulting from the use of the information contained herein.

All rights reserved. No part of this publication may be reproduced, stored in a retrieval system or transmitted in any form or by any means, electronic, mechanical, photocopying, recording or otherwise without the express written permission of the publisher.

Publisher: CCB Publishing
             British Columbia, Canada
             www.ccbpublishing.com

Dedication

I am dedicating this book to my girlfriend, Hope Heritz, who I truly adore. Thank you for your encouragement and valuable insight.

Acknowledgements

This book is a sequel to my first book entitled, *The Last Assignment*, published in December 2013.

Special thanks to Doug and Jeannine Schrock, who graciously invited me to stay with them in St. Croix. During that visit I became inspired to write my first novel. Thanks to my friends, Gary Cochrane and Roger Sellers, for providing some of the Vietnam War background information. Kevin Sheets, I thank you for your continued encouragement. Also, I would like to acknowledge and thank Tammy Landers, my editor, and Paul Rabinovitch, CCB Publishing, my publisher.

Books by John W. Gemmer

The Last Assignment

Harsh Consequences

Prologue

Dominic Ricci, the prominent, long-time Mafia boss of Detroit, Michigan, sat awaiting his fate in the holding cell of the Wayne County Jail. He did not appreciate being treated by the authorities as if he were a common criminal. Instead, Ricci knew he was a man to be respected, served, and feared. For well over sixty years, he and his father controlled organized crime in Michigan through business connections, politics, law enforcement, and the judicial system.

In the cell across from Ricci, were about a half-dozen, low-level criminals waiting to be processed to more permanent lockup facilities upstairs. All of the men were repeat offenders, accustomed to the standard jail procedures.

Dressed in a dark suit, silk tie, and Italian loafers, Ricci looked and felt out of place. His cellmates wore various types of clothing, depicting their obvious meager states of existence. When Ricci was first brought in, several derogatory remarks were directed towards him by some ill-informed criminals, who were unaware of his status. However, those comments ended abruptly after several of the detainees overheard a jail officer call Ricci by his full name.

Ricci had been locked up for several hours, and he was upset the guards had not offered him a drink, a smoke, or at the very least, something to eat. He thought he should have been afforded more respect and consideration than his jailers were providing him. He had repeatedly asked for a soda and was told he would not be getting anything until after he was either bailed out or assigned to a permanent cell.

That morning the County Prosecutor had issued a warrant for Ricci's arrest, accusing him of masterminding the kidnapping and attempted murder of Louis Stroh, the Michigan State Senate leader, and Anne Bishop, his secretary/girlfriend. The warrant was based on evidence provided by Henry Wallace, Ricci's former attorney, and an anonymous person who claimed to be the hit man.

Wallace had agreed to testify against Ricci in return for his freedom, immunity from prosecution, and indefinite governmental protection for himself and his family.

The hit man had sent a cassette tape along with a short note, supposedly tying Ricci to the crime. The note was hand written and claimed that Wallace had hired him (the anonymous professional killer) to do the job for the Ricci Family, or the Detroit Partnership, as it became known.

Across town, Paul Minello, the underboss for the Ricci Family, immediately hired Gordon Rosenfeld, a well-known criminal defense attorney, to represent Ricci. Rosenfeld had assured Minello that the Boss would be out of jail before the end of the day.

With every passing minute, Ricci became more frustrated and angry, as he waited for his release. His thoughts drifted to how he was going to personally orchestrate the death of Henry Wallace, regardless, if he ever testified against him or not.

Ricci demanded loyalty from all his men. Years earlier, when Wallace had become the Family attorney, Ricci remembered telling him he expected absolute loyalty and that anything less would be dealt with harshly. Testifying against a mob boss would never be condoned, without very serious consequences to the perpetrator. When Ricci learned about Wallace's intent to testify against him, he immediately ordered a hit.

A mole in the Prosecutor's Office had informed Ricci about Wallace and the existence of a tape recording, where Wallace and the hit man were discussing the particulars of the premeditated murder of Stroh. The recording had been sent to the authorities via the United States mail.

Ricci knew he had never talked with the hit man, and he was hopeful the recording would not be enough to implicate him in the crime. He planned to deny any involvement, or knowledge, of the criminal events surrounding the Stroh case, and would claim never to have authorized or sanctioned any such preposterous activity. He intended to blame Wallace for everything.

An informant in the Detroit Police Department had told Ricci the information on the tape recording never mentioned his name. Considering the facts, Ricci thought any good criminal defense attorney should be able to keep him from being prosecuted for the crime. However, in the event of a trial, Ricci knew there would always be a juror or two he could sway.

Ricci reasoned the hit man must have known beforehand about their plan to double-cross him. He presumed this to be the reason the hit man had decided to double-cross them instead, and to provide the authorities with the cassette recording. Ricci believed Cavallaro had talked in order to save his own skin. If he could prove it, Ricci knew he would have to kill him.

Nevertheless, Cavallaro continued to insist that he had not told anyone about their plans, including the hit man. And, he claimed, he had lost his finger because he was unwilling to talk, in order to protect the Family. He credited the business owner, whose arrival unexpectedly spooked the hit man, with saving his life. Ricci doubted his explanation, but could not disprove it without more information. He knew it would be a bad idea to kill his cousin's only son, Tony, without proving that he had betrayed the Family.

Once we find the hit man, I will have him roughed up for a while, before I interrogate him myself. No doubt the truth will ultimately emerge. If I find out it was Tony who betrayed us, I will have him shot first, before the hit man gets it. I would want to send a frightening message to all Ricci Family members and associates; no one will ever lie to me or screw me over again and live to talk about it

Ricci was extremely embarrassed about being in jail. Neither he nor his father had ever been inside a jail cell before, at least for very long. It was an experience Ricci had always dodged due to Wallace's superior legal skills.

In the past, the Riccis' had always managed to get the

cooperation of the authorities, mostly through intimidation or bribery. That cooperation was the main reason the Riccis' nefarious criminal activities including gambling, loansharking, extortion, narcotics, and labor racketeering, along with the many legitimate businesses they owned, continued to thrive and prosper.

Nevertheless, this case was different because the Partnership had attempted to murder the Speaker of the Michigan House. There was far too much media attention surrounding the case and in no way could it be overlooked or forgotten. Ricci knew somebody was going to be held responsible for the crime and was hopeful it would not be him.

All those payoffs seem like a waste of time and money now, he thought. I'm sitting in this smelly shit hole waiting to be released. I'm tired, anxious, and hungry. What I'd really like is a good steak, a shot of booze, and a couple hours with one of those lovely French Canadian hookers I know in Windsor.

I wonder what Wallace and the hit man are thinking about right now. They know the right amount of cash can buy anyone or anything. They should know my power and reach are almost infinite. They can't hide from me forever. When I get out of here, I'm not going to rest until those two bastards are dead.

Chapter 1

Just before sunset, Jim Bartlett was sitting on his front porch drinking a beer and admiring the picturesque views of the Caribbean. He was waiting for his girlfriend, Moira Gray, who was showering and would be joining him shortly. Bartlett leaned back in his rocker, closed his eyes, and thought about his past. More than twenty-five years ago he had begun his career as a professional killer for the Mafia.

I'm finally going to be able to enjoy a secluded and peaceful life because I've worked out an ingenious retirement plan, he thought. I'm no longer going to be a paid assassin. Instead, I'll be a small businessman and a respected member of the St. Croix community.

Bartlett wanted to retire early for several reasons. They included: a desire to get married, to enjoy his money, to avoid being killed by his former employers, and to retire safely on a tropical island. He and Moira, it appeared, were well on their way to making some of those dreams a reality. Furthermore, Bartlett was beginning to doubt his ability to continue working and survive as a professional killer.

Nevertheless, he was not changing himself because of some lofty sense of morality. No, his unexpected metamorphosis was self-induced for his benefit, and self-preservation, only.

Consciously, Bartlett had been thinking about his prior activities as a hit man. Those thoughts reminded him of his vulnerability. There were still people from New Orleans and Detroit looking for him, whether he was retired or not. And Bartlett knew, once the Chicago Outfit and their affiliated New York crime family, in particular, realized he had quit working, they would not be too happy with him either. He knew he would always be at risk, and if Moira was with him, she would be at risk too. The situation concerned him. He was prepared to protect himself but she was not. In fact, she was not even aware of her own vulnerability. Bartlett hoped that he could always protect her from his past, but he understood nothing was ever certain.

The squeak of the front door opening interrupted his thoughts. Moira appeared dressed in a revealing, black, silk-laced negligée and robe. She sat down in the adjacent rocker and took a sip of his beer. "What a beautiful evening," she said. "Thank you."

Bartlett smiled and said, "Thanks for sharing the day with me too. You look relaxed."

"Very," she said. "It's so peaceful here."

"You know Moira, I've dreamt about this moment for a long time, and I'm happy you're finally here. I hope you're happy too," he said, smiling at her.

"I am," she said, earnestly.

Bartlett arose, grasped her hands, and slowly pulled her up and into his arms. "You look very lovely and sexy this evening," he said, as he hugged her and tenderly kissed her lips.

She passionately kissed him back and quickly realized he had become aroused. Moira thought that under the circumstances, Bartlett would naturally want them to go to bed. "Not now Jimmy," she said, trying to temporarily delay the inevitable. Let's wait a while; the sun will be setting shortly."

"There will always be sunsets like this for us to share Moira. I want to make love to you now," he insisted, holding her more closely in his arms.

"Soon," she promised, looking fondly into his eyes. "Let's enjoy the sunset first. Besides, we have the rest of the night to make love."

"If you didn't look so damn gorgeous in that outfit, I might be more patient and willing to wait," Bartlett said, as he slowly lifted her robe and negligee, exposing her black lace panties.

Moira shifted nervously and said, "Jimmy, someone might be watching us. Maybe you shouldn't ..."

"Nobody can see us up here," he assured her.

"Are you certain?" she asked.

"Yes, it's like my own little world, up on this hill."

She waited several seconds, smiled and said, "Ok, we'll do it your way this time. Let's go to bed."

"You won't be disappointed," he said, very convincingly. "Afterwards, I'll give you a great massage."

"I hope so because you won't be disappointed either," Moira said, teasing him with a very sexy and seductive smile, as she went inside the house.

Bartlett followed her, closed the front door, and began removing his clothing, as he approached the bedroom door. The soothing noise of the surf, and the soft romantic music permeating from the living room, set the perfect mood for their love-making. Bartlett made love to her passionately and rhythmically, as if he were playing a priceless Stradivarius. Afterwards, she lay in his arms satisfied, as they both drifted off to sleep.

* * *

Rays of sunlight poured into the bedroom Saturday morning. They had slept soundly and Bartlett had awakened early to make breakfast. Eventually, Moira wandered out to the kitchen for a cup of tea. "How did you sleep?" he asked.

"Fine," she said. "It's so peaceful here. I'm beginning to understand why you love it."

"Our lifestyle is a lot slower in the islands," he said. "I used to enjoy the hustle and bustle of Chicago but not anymore."

"I've noticed. What time are we going to Buck Island National Park?"

"I'd like to get there by ten-thirty," he said. "We should be getting ready to go pretty soon."

"I can be ready anytime," she said.

Bartlett planned for them to swim, snorkel, and enjoy the pristine Buck Island beach during the day. In the evening, he wanted to take Moira to his favorite restaurant for dinner.

Bartlett loved visiting the tiny island and wanted Moira to experience the sights of the various aquatic animals on the reef. Thirty minutes later, the couple arrived at a local marina not far from Buck Island, where Bartlett rented a small powerboat and snorkeling equipment. It was a beautiful sunny day. Moira marveled at the different shades of blues and greens in the glistening water. She was thankful for the calmness of the seas as they hastily motored to the National Park.

Upon their arrival, they decided to sunbathe on the beach for an hour before swimming out to the reef. A cable ran along the reef making the tour easier for less experienced swimmers like Moira. She was particularly amazed by the many colorful creatures that congregated there.

Bartlett had packed a small cooler with food and cold

drinks. After noon, they located an isolated area on the island, where they ate, talked, and embraced. Late in the afternoon, they gathered their possessions, loaded the boat, and departed for the shore. Bartlett gave Moira a quick water-side tour of the Christiansted side of St. Croix before heading back to the marina.

After they got back to the Jeep, Moira smiled at Bartlett, wrapped her arms around his waist, and gave him an adoring hug and kiss. "Jimmy," she said appreciatively, "thank you for a wonderful day. Buck Island is a very special place."

"You can stay in St. Croix forever," he said, after they had exchanged several more kisses. "We can get married here and I'll take good care of you. After the honeymoon, we can go back to the States and settle your affairs. What do you say?"

Moira stared at him intently, hesitated and said, "I want to stay but there are so many things to consider. First, I need to go back to Chicago. I told my boss I'd be back to work on Monday morning. He was extremely nice to let me use the remainder of my vacation time, to be here with you. Let's talk more tonight during dinner. There are some things I'd like to tell you."

"Alright," Bartlett said, sensing some apprehension from her. "Maybe I'm pushing you a little too hard and maybe too fast but you know that's the way I am."

"I know," she said.

"I just want to make sure you know how I feel."

"I already have a pretty good idea Jimmy. Why not talk about it tonight," she suggested.

"Okay honey," he said, trying not to look too discouraged. "I need to check in at the shop before we head home. I'll introduce you to the employee who helps me run the shop when I'm gone. I think you'll like her."

"Oh okay, I'd like to see your business and meet your employee. But, you never told me you had anything other than a home on the island," she said, with a confused look on her face. "How long have you owned the shop?"

"Almost a year I guess. Gee, I'm sorry and just a little perplexed. I thought I had mentioned the business to you, a year ago, when I first opened," Bartlett said.

"I don't ever remember you telling me," she said.

"Sorry, I thought I did but forgetfulness is indicative of my age," he said, with a slight grin.

"Well, maybe you did and I just didn't hear you," she said.

I'm sure he never mentioned the business to me. He is always so secretive about things. It's probably because of his experience in following governmental procedures. There is no need to make a big deal about it now.

Fifteen minutes later, they arrived at Bartlett's shop, located in the center of Christiansted. Moira noted "The Ursula Shop" sign on the front of the building. Bartlett drove around to the back and parked. Moira immediately noticed a slender, full-breasted, younger woman standing behind one of the front display counters, upon entering the shop.

The women exchanged quick glances before Bartlett said to Moira, "I'd like to introduce you to Rosa."

Moira failed to extend her hand but gave the attractive woman another look and said, "Hello," along with a half-smile and a nod.

"Rosa, this is my girlfriend, Moira. She's been visiting me for the past week," announced Bartlett.

"It's very nice to meet you Moira, but Mr. Bartlett never mentioned you, or that you would be coming for a visit. How long have you two been dating?"

"We've been together for well over two years," Moira said.

"How long will you be here?" Rosa asked.

"Two more days, then I have to go home."

"Where's home?" Rosa inquired.

"Evanston, Illinois, just outside of Chicago."

"How do you like St. Croix?"

"It's very beautiful," Moira said.

"Yes, it is. And, Chicago is a very long way from here. What a shame," said Rosa. "St. Croix is a very romantic place."

"Yes, I know! I hope to return soon. Nice to meet you," Moira said abruptly.

"Yes ... nice to meet you too," Rosa said, as she

continued to stare, conspicuously, at the older woman.

Bartlett noted Moira's face had become slightly flushed after Rosa began questioning her.

He wondered why Rosa appeared to be conducting a mini-interrogation of his girlfriend, instead of them just having a casual conversation. What is going on, he wondered?

After observing some more unspoken tension between the two women, Bartlett nonchalantly took Moira's hand and led her towards his office. "Back here is my office," he said, awkwardly.

Several minutes later, the couple emerged and Bartlett said to Rosa, "We're leaving now. You can call me at home if anything important comes up."

"If I need anything, I certainly will call you," she said, smiling brightly at him.

"Bye," Moira said, pretending to be politely engaging as she stared at the woman's left hand. Moira noticed there was neither an engagement ring nor a wedding ring on her finger.

Moira trusted Bartlett but she wondered if she could trust the woman working for him. Rosa dressed plainly but her perfume selection seemed to Moira to have a very enticing scent. Moira thought, the woman's features, and long dark hair, made her appear intriguing, exotic, and sexy.

What does Jimmy really think about her? Does he have feelings for her too, wondered Moira.

Bartlett wondered why both women were acting a bit standoffish. What's going on? Could both women be slightly jealous of each other's relationship with me? I know Rosa likes me as a boss, but judging from Moira's reaction to meeting her, I wonder if she thinks Rosa has a plan for me romantically. I don't think she does, but there was a time when I would have welcomed those feelings. I hope Moira doesn't think I am being unfaithful to her with Rosa. Maybe women just don't appreciate other women being around their men. He decided that now was not the right time to ask.

* * *

The Seafood Bistro was a small and charming local restaurant, recessed into the side of a cliff, overlooking the Caribbean. The eatery was pricey but comparable to the other outdoor dining places in Christiansted.

Bartlett had made a reservation timed just before sunset and had requested a table nearest the railing, overlooking the shore. The restaurant was intoxicating with its coastal views and the sounds of the surf slowly crashing and returning to the sea. When they entered the restaurant, the unmistakable voice of Julio Iglesias singing "The Girl from Ipanema" was softly broadcast throughout the grounds.

The maître d' immediately greeted them and escorted them to a charming little table, where a bottle of Dom Perignon was already being chilled. "Thank you," Bartlett said, as they were seated.

"You're welcome sir. Jeffrey will be taking care of you this evening. If there is anything else you need, please let us know."

"I will, but everything looks perfect," Bartlett said.

"Would you like me to pour the champagne?" offered the maître d'.

"No, I can handle it from here, but thanks," Bartlett said. After the maître d' departed, Bartlett asked Moira if she liked the restaurant.

"It's very nice, and the views are breathtaking, but it looks expensive. You don't need to do this for me," she said, almost blushing.

"I know I don't, but this evening is very special, and I wanted to arrange a romantic dinner that you'd never forget," Bartlett said.

"Well, you have succeeded admirably. This has already been such a wonderful day that I will never forget. I've had so much fun since coming to St. Croix."

"I'm glad," he said, as he showed her the champagne.

After Bartlett poured their drinks and offered an affectionate toast to Moira, he stated, "I know you have reservations about getting married, quitting your job, and moving here. If you want to get a job in Christiansted, I'm sure there are lawyers who would appreciate your experience."

"Perhaps, but I doubt it," she said. "St. Croix is a very

beautiful and wonderful place. I know you are happy here but I'm not sure if I could be happy here too. The island is very small and isolated. All of my friends and family are back in the States. Besides, I am used to big-city living. Before I give you an answer, I want to go back to Chicago and think more about what I am doing. I want us to be married but quitting my job and moving to St. Croix is a big decision too."

Bartlett nodded as he intently listened to Moira's comments. When she finished talking, he said, "I'm not surprised to hear your reservations, and I understand your concern. I realize St. Croix would be a very big change for you, but I think you should give it a chance. In time, island living can become very enjoyable, peaceful, and addicting. I realize I shouldn't be putting too much pressure on you, but I am anxious to know your decision. However, I am willing to give you all the time you need, because I don't want to risk losing you."

"You aren't going to lose me," she said. "I love you, but I don't want to feel pressured this time around."

"Moira, I'm sorry about being overly aggressive and too serious. I really didn't intend to be that way, but you know how I am."

"I know, but those are some of the things I like about you," she said. "If it's alright with you, I'd rather not discuss this anymore. I want us to enjoy the rest of our time together. If I can give you an answer within a month, would that be acceptable to you?"

"Sure," he said, immediately trying to appear satisfied

with the compromise. "That'll be fine. I need to come to the States in about three weeks anyway. I have some business matters to conclude. We can talk then."

"Yes, that would be fine," she answered. "Besides, I would hope that three weeks isn't too long to wait."

"No, it's not too long."

"I don't have to remind you, we do have the rest of our lives to be together," she said grinning.

"Yes, you're right, we do," said Bartlett.

"Good, let's enjoy dinner and the rest of the evening, honey," said Moira.

"Alright, I can do that," Bartlett said, smiling. "Would you like another glass of champagne before dinner?"

"Yes, that would be great. You know Jimmy, if I didn't know you well enough, I might think you were trying to get me drunk to take advantage of me later tonight."

"That was not my intention. However, it does sound intriguing. What do you think?"

"I guess you'll just have to wait and see," she said, with a mischievous and rather naughty expression on her face.

Chapter 2

Early Sunday morning, Moira boarded a flight to Miami that included an afternoon connection into Chicago.

She had concluded a week-long vacation with Bartlett in St. Croix and two weeks prior to that, she had been vacationing in Saugatuck, Michigan. Vacations were always rejuvenating and fun, but Moira was ready to go back to work. She could only imagine the stacks of paperwork waiting on her desk.

Also, Moira needed more time to think about Bartlett's proposal. The two people she most often relied upon for advice were Pauline Hadley, her closest friend, and Sarah Sloan, her therapist. She had made a mental note to contact both women upon her return to Evanston. Moira was hopeful the ladies would offer some objective opinions concerning her marriage plans, employment, and relocation to St. Croix.

Prior to her departure, Bartlett promised he would call her every other day in order to stay in touch. Thirty minutes into the flight, Moira was already looking forward to his calls. She realized she would be completely alone in Chicago without him. When they parted, she felt as if she were leaving part of herself behind. It was sad going back to the States without Jimmy. However, his absence was somewhat of a relief, allowing her the time to decide whether or not she would accept his proposal.

Moira knew she wanted to get married and share her life with him, but her prior marriage had ended in a disaster. Divorce was an experience she never wanted to repeat. Frankly, the idea of a second marriage, even with the perfect man, scared her.

The flight had been underway for a while, when the stewardess offered her a beverage. Moira selected a glass of red wine and pushed her seat back to relax and reminisce about her past.

She had grown up on a 40-acre farm in Iowa, which had been in the Gray family for generations. The farm was minimally profitable, and the implements were old and needed repair. They grew corn and wheat, but the meager income was hardly enough to justify continuing to farm the land.

Her mother, Nancy Gray, worked in a grain processing plant in town and her father, Ronald Gray, worked as a mechanic at the Rushville Ford dealership along with farming their land. Silvia, her only sibling, had died at age 12 from a pneumonia outbreak.

Ronald was a heavy drinker and often came home late after partying at the local tavern. It was rumored he had another woman on the side, but there was never any proof to substantiate the claim.

Moira led a quiet existence and had only a few really close friends. She always enjoyed Sundays at the Catholic Church, where she mingled with the other kids after Mass. However, most of her long-time school friends departed Rushville after high school graduation, in search of a job, military service, or higher education.

Living on a small and isolated rural farm was hard, and much was expected from her. The family was somewhat sequestered, because they only had one car, and received infrequent visits from family and friends. Her aunts and uncles were elderly and either lived alone or in the local senior center. The Grays had few family reunions and, for the most part, kept to themselves.

Moira had been an excellent student and felt fortunate to have attended the small Catholic community college twenty-five miles from her home. She graduated with an associate degree in business, financed by a student loan program.

After graduation, Moira had planned to move to Des Moines, rent an apartment, and pursue a business career. However, her plans were altered after her father's disappearance on June 9, 1972. Ronald had been seen partying at the tavern earlier that evening and failed to come home. He was never seen or heard from again. Moira imagined he had hooked up with a woman and had left the state. She remembered he had always talked about moving out west and wondered if he had finally done it. Moira referred to his absence as the "famous disappearing act."

After her father had disappeared, Moira decided to stay in Rushville with her distraught mother, aging aunts, and uncles. Three years later, her mother moved in with an older man, deciding it was time to move on with her life.

At age 23, Moira decided to leave her hometown and pursue her original plans. She moved to Des Moines and, after only three weeks, met her future husband, Larry Sanders, at a Catholic Church fellowship event.

They dated for over six months before he asked her to marry him. At the time, Moira believed she loved him, and decided foolishly to give marriage a try. At first, their marriage seemed secure and Moira was very happy. But after several years, they began to argue and fight, mostly about money and her desire to have children.

Larry was a real estate salesman for the largest realty firm in town. Previously, he had been married but for less than a year. No children resulted from that marriage. He struggled with sales and produced sub-par commissions.

Moira worked as a payables clerk for a local manufacturing firm. Her income frequently exceeded his, and she was the bread winner for the family.

They purchased a small bungalow in a quiet neighborhood. Moira invested her entire life's savings into a sizable down payment on the home. When they divorced, she was angry and shocked to find out Larry was entitled to half the proceeds from the sale of the house. Afterwards, Moira vowed to never put her hard earned assets in jeopardy again.

When the divorce was final, Moira moved away from Des Moines and Larry too. She relocated to Chicago and accepted a position with Karp, Gutman, and Bell, a local, medium-sized law firm. Prior to her promotion to office manager, she worked ten years as a business clerk, handling payables and receivables. She rented an apartment just outside the Loop, but after her promotion, she purchased a 1,100 sq. ft. older home in Evanston.

Moira decided, if she ever remarried, she would sell the house and invest the proceeds in a retirement account for herself. Her boss convinced her to insist on a pre-nuptial agreement prior to any future marriage plans, to keep any future spouse from getting half of her assets again.

* * *

It was early evening before Moira got home from O'Hare airport. It had been a long day and she was tired. She made herself a quick supper, got into bed, and scanned a magazine to relax. She wanted to be rested and mentally ready for an extremely busy Monday.

* * *

Sunday evening, Bartlett went out for dinner. He made an early reservation at The Salty Pirate because he wanted to eat, drink, and unwind before the crowds arrived. He missed Moira, but the idea he would be sharing his life with her, was a bit unsettling. Love seemed like a crazed emotion, almost like insanity to him.

Once Moira had left to go back to Chicago, Bartlett began to realize the consequences of falling in love. He began to experience an unanticipated feeling of loneliness without her there. Bartlett had experienced loneliness before, but he had always relied on casual relationships (one night stands) to placate his feelings.

He was aware of another strange feeling, namely a sudden concern for someone other than himself. After all, as a long-time bachelor, it was unusual to feel the need to care about women for anything other than sex and some limited companionship. Bartlett was beginning to understand that love and marriage would probably change a lot of things in his life.

The Salty Pirate was busy for a Sunday evening. Bartlett was happy with his reserved table, outside on the patio overlooking the beach. He quickly ordered a drink and a favorite meal.

As he sipped his drink, he began to reminisce about his past family life. He was born in 1950 to Stan and Marie Bartkowski, near Cracow, Poland. They named him after his father's brother, John. However, the name he had been using for the last several years was Jim Bartlett.

The Bartkowski family was the typical hard working Polish family. When Bartkowski was eight years old, his parents entered the country through Ellis Island, like many other poor, Polish immigrants. They first settled in

Brooklyn but quickly migrated to Chicago, where his dad worked in an East Chicago foundry. His mother was a home-maker and raised him, and his 3-year-old brother Steve, with an iron hand. The family never acquired many possessions but they were not destitute either.

He enlisted in the United States Army during the Vietnam War, even though it would have been more preferable in 1968 to have attended college. Regardless, he had done alright without a college education. He had plenty of money (from his career as a professional killer), a nice home, and a profitable small business. Not too bad for a poor immigrant kid.

Bartlett recalled basic training at Ft. Leonard Wood, Missouri and advanced training at Ft. Benning, Georgia. Those drill instructors were assholes most of the time. My folks were very proud of my service in Vietnam and my advancement from Private to Sergeant in less than two years.

He remembered being injured, but not permanently, during the war. Bartlett was thankful for the base camp medical facility and the life-saving care he had received from the Army doctors and nurses.

Bartlett remembered how impressed his Mother had been by the number of service medals the military had awarded him. He was surprised the Commanding Officer had given him a medal for saving Second Lieutenant David Coles' life. After all, it was his job to protect the men in his platoon.

When dinner was served, Bartlett put his remembrances

about the past temporarily on hold. After dinner he began to reflect again, in particular, about when his Mother had died. Bartlett realized that upon her death, he was totally alone.

When he and Moira talked about getting married, he was hopeful a spouse would help to replace the loss of his Mother, which was a serious void in his life. It was a comforting feeling to realize that soon there would be someone special for him, once again.

He had loved his family and missed having them in his life, but it would have been very challenging to have kept his professional career hidden from them long-term. They would have had too many questions. Bartlett was glad he did not have to hide his career from them anymore.

Retirement seemed to be agreeing with him. He was glad to be out of the business and happy there were no further assignments to complete. At times he missed the work, but his life as a paid killer was over. He was opening a new door and closing another, with the permanent addition of Moira into his life. Bartlett was recognizing his life was slowly beginning to change, and for the better.

His journey from John Bartkowski to John Moore, then to Emery Clements, and now to Jim Bartlett, had not been an easy task. During his criminal career, spanning several decades, he had used many aliases for business, travel, freelance opportunities, and concealment purposes.

John Bartkowski, now known as Jim Bartlett, had been a serious, purposefully driven man, who planned his assignments with precision. Now, he had effectively planned his retirement too. After a lifetime of work, he was prepared to reap the benefits of a new life. He had skillfully created a way for John Bartkowski to evolve into Jim Bartlett; a man of leisure, a respectable businessman, and a family man. Bartlett knew he would soon be almost devoid of his violent past.

A smile appeared on his face as he thought about the voyage he had taken to get to his current position. He had made it almost unscathed. Generally speaking, he had no regrets.

His work as a contractual killer never bothered him, despite the fact that society would always consider him a sociopath. Nevertheless, he considered himself to be an honorable and fair-minded businessman, who was well-paid to perform a valuable service for important people. Bartlett considered his hits to be comparable to ordinary work, just like anyone else who was gainfully employed. He believed the people whom he killed were probably very deserving of their fate.

Ever since he had left Vietnam, he knew he was devoid of a normal conscience. The terrible consequences, and realities of war, had forever changed his way of thinking.

Although, sometimes he did regret the collateral damage he had inflicted on the innocent, who would occasionally get in the way. But, it was part of the job, unfortunate but necessary.

After several drinks and a good meal, Bartlett drove home. He would call Moira to make sure she had arrived safely, watch some television, and retire for the evening.

When he got home, the phone was ringing as he opened the back door. He anticipated it would be Moira, so he answered. "Hi honey! How was the flight?"

"Hi Mr. Bartlett," the voice responded.

Immediately, he recognized Rosa as the caller, and he wondered what she wanted this late on a Sunday evening.

"Hey, what's wrong? Are you alright?" Bartlett asked.

"Oh, I'm fine," said Rosa.

"Well, that's good; I was worried when I heard your voice. I'm kind of embarrassed by the "honey" comment. I was expecting a call from my girlfriend. She left to go back to Chicago today."

"That's okay, I understand," she said. "I just wanted to apologize for being a little strange the other day in the shop. You know, when you introduced me to your friend."

"Why do you think you were acting strangely?"

Hesitating briefly, Rosa said, "Well, I'm sorry for my behavior. Ever since my husband has been gone, I sometimes get confused. I guess I've been kind of lonely too. Sometimes, it would be nice to have someone to talk with. Well, I guess uh … I just got nervous thinking you were going to replace me, when you brought her into the shop."

"I'm sorry you felt threatened, but I have no plans to replace you."

"That's a relief to know," she said. "The shop has become a big part of my life and it's nice that you're there too."

"Well, I'm glad you enjoy your job, and I'm happy you're at the shop."

"Will you be coming in tomorrow morning Mr. Bartlett?"

"Yes around ten," he said.

"Maybe we can talk more then," she said, nervously.

"Yes, maybe," he said. "I'll see you in the morning Rosa. Goodnight."

"Goodnight Mr. Bartlett."

"Rosa, you can call me Jim if you want. I'll see you in the morning."

"Okay, goodnight Jim," she said sweetly.

After hanging up the telephone Bartlett began thinking about their conversation.

What was that call all about? I wonder what's really going on in her mind. Does she want to have a personal relationship with me? If I were not involved with Moira, I might be willing to give her a try. Well, maybe I would. Better forget about it though, unless Moira changes her mind. It's probably not such a good idea to be mixing business and pleasure.

Chapter 3

Monday afternoon, Moira called Pauline Hadley, her best friend. "Hey, I'm back," she said.

"How was the trip?"

"Okay. I had a good time. St. Croix is a very beautiful place, but it's small and isolated."

"Well honey, what did you expect? It's an island in the middle of the Caribbean, isn't it?

"Yes, but I thought it might have been a little bigger. After driving around for a few days, it isn't as big as one might think."

"You sound like you had a nice time, but you don't really seem overly excited."

"Well, I'm not and that's a problem. It was really fun being there but it's good to be home. I've got a backlog of work to do at the office."

"I know what you mean," said Pauline. "I'm always busier before and after I return from vacation too."

"Want to come for dinner tonight?"

"Sure, I don't have any plans. What time do you want me?"

"Seven o'clock will be fine. I'd like to talk about my situation. I'm confused and I need help sorting some things out," Moira admitted.

"Is something wrong with you and Jimmy?"

"No, it's just the whole thing. The situation seems to be closing in on me, and I'm really nervous. Jimmy is great! We had a really good time, and St. Croix is a very exotic, fun, and picturesque place."

"Well, what's the problem then?"

"Oh, I don't know. Maybe I am making more out of this than I should. I'll tell you the whole story tonight. I've got to get back to work."

"Okay honey. I'll see you at seven."

* * *

Promptly at seven, Pauline arrived at Moira's front door. She knocked several times but there was no answer, so she cracked the door open and shouted, "Hey Moira, are you here?"

Moira appeared from the kitchen and said, "Come on in Pauline, I'm back here. Our dinner is almost ready."

"Whatever you're cooking, it smells really great!"

"I hope you like pot roast."

"I'm sure I will," Pauline said.

After dinner, Pauline and Moira adjourned to the living room sofa and began to talk about Moira's personal life.

"What exactly is troubling you honey?" asked Pauline.

"As you know, Jimmy asked me to marry him and I accepted. Now I am having second thoughts."

"Really, why?"

"Well, I love him and I think he feels the same about me, but how can I be sure? I don't want to make another mistake!"

"Unfortunately honey, there is no way to know until after you have been married for a while. What do your instincts tell you?"

"I feel like I'm ready to be married again, but I'm still a little worried."

"I know you're nervous, but I'd say go with your instincts. Relationships are never totally predictable, as I'm sure your therapist has told you."

"We've talked extensively about relationships and the complexity of marriage. Men can change once the honeymoon is over and not always for the best."

"Is Jimmy like your ex-husband?"

"No, Jimmy is a totally independent, caring, mature, and responsible man. Larry was a very needy, immature young man when we got married. In fairness, I was too young, naïve, and foolish myself, to have been married."

"You're not anymore. What else is bothering you?"

"I'd have to move to St. Croix if we got married."

"Why can't you stay in Chicago?"

"He has an established business there and he wants to stay rather than move back to the States. I don't know if I would be happy living in St. Croix without my friends. I worry that I might feel lonely and isolated."

"I understand sweetie," Pauline said.

"Once I moved to St. Croix, I'd have to quit my job. I can't decide whether I would want to continue working or not. I doubt I could find a comparable job in Christiansted."

"Sounds like you have gotten yourself into quite a dilemma. Would he be willing to compromise?'

"I'm sure he would be willing to, but he just started the business a year ago."

"Honey, is it really that important to you if he's unable to compromise right now? You could look at this move as kind of an adventure. It would be a new start for the both of you."

"I never thought of it that way before."

"If you decided to move to St. Croix would that be so bad? Is it a deal breaker?"

"I don't know. That's one of my concerns, I guess. It's what I'm considering."

"You told me you love him, right?"

"Yes, I do love him."

"Does it really matter that much to you where you live, as long as you're together?"

"I don't think it should," Moira said. "One positive aspect of the move would be it doesn't seem to matter to him if I work or not. In fact, I think he would prefer I didn't."

"Some women might consider that as a big plus, if you know what I mean."

"I know. If I knew this marriage was going to last, I'd probably enjoy living a life of leisure for a while," she said, laughingly. "Seriously though, I need to be concerned about my retirement, in the event of another divorce. Besides, I don't want to have to split my assets with anyone again."

"Get a pre-nup if it bothers you that much. He would sign it, wouldn't he?"

"I'm sure he would if I told him that would be a condition of our getting married or not," said Moira. "But, we've already had this discussion before, and I am pretty sure he is okay with a pre-nup. He might ask me to sign one too."

"It sounds like you have thought about most of the details honey. You just need to sit down and talk to Jimmy about the things that are really troubling you. Afterwards, you can decide what you want to do. If things can be worked out for your mutual satisfaction, go ahead and get married. That's the best advice I can give you."

"Thanks for listening Pauline," said Moira.

"Okay honey, glad to help you any time. Hey, it's late and we both have to go to work tomorrow. I've got to run. I need my beauty sleep you know. Thanks for dinner."

Pauline got up from the couch, hugged Moira, and hurried toward the door. "Call if you want to talk again," she said.

"Thanks," said Moira. "I'll keep you posted."

Fifteen minutes later, Moira finished washing the dishes, cleaning up the kitchen, and headed for her bedroom. She appreciated Pauline's friendship and valued her advice. Moira got into bed and tried to sleep. Unfortunately, the discussion of marriage, and the move, were keeping her awake.

Pauline is right! I have to think this through, talk to Jimmy, and decide what to do. I will be the one suffering the consequences, if I make another mistake. But I know Jimmy is the right man for me. If I want to be with him, what does it matter where I live or whether I am employed or not? He says he loves me and will take care of me, and I believe him. I guess I should get married, move to St. Croix, and enjoy the rest of my life. However, Jimmy must absolutely promise to permanently end his involvement with the United States government. If not, our marriage plans, and our relationship, will be in jeopardy. I could never tolerate another extended period of separation from him, like before.

Chapter 4

The City of Commerce Township, on the upper west side of Detroit, is a small and sheltered area from the massive, often hostile, environment encompassing much of the metropolitan area.

Upper middle class families reside in the old and new neighborhoods there, intertwined with lake-front properties and nearby to several private country clubs.

In one of the older, yet elegant, two-story, lake properties, lived Ashley Jenkins, the wife of Dr. Peter Jenkins, a well-known psychiatrist. Ashley was the only child of Henry Wallace, a prominent local attorney and his wife, Helen, now deceased.

Ashley and her husband Peter are long-time residents of Commerce Township and the Detroit area. The couple had a twelve-year-old daughter, named Ruth Anne. Ashley was a homemaker, just like her deceased mother had been for many years. She grew up in a very affluent household in the exclusive part of Gross Point, Michigan, northeast of Detroit. Ashley felt fortunate that her husband was able to continue providing her with the life she had grown accustomed to with her parents.

It had been almost a month since the Prosecutor had begun safeguarding Ashley's family, with the help of the local police. She had been shocked when she learned her Dad's practice involved working for Dominic Ricci, the boss of the Detroit Partnership crime family. Wallace, and his immediate family, had been promised protection until it was no longer deemed necessary, depending on the outcome of Ricci's trial.

Ashley was concerned but reasoned that Ricci would not be as likely to bother with them, once the trial was completed.

Two plainclothes officers had been assigned to guard the Jenkins family from inside their home, and two uniformed officers were in a squad car, on a daily basis, in front of their residence. A female officer had been assigned to escort Ruth Anne to and from her elementary school. However, Jenkins declined any assistance from the police but carried a .40-caliber Glock, for his own protection.

Occasionally, Ashley would receive a phone call from her father. On those occasions, she would have a chance to communicate her concern, and her disappointment, that he had placed their family in such a compromising situation. Ashley wanted to be able to resume a normal life as soon as possible. She could hardly wait for her Dad to testify, so this ordeal would be behind them. She worried about her family's safety and, to a lesser degree, her father's. Ashley wondered why a brilliant and experienced attorney would ever consider working for a man like Ricci. She thought he should have known better.

After dinner, Ashley was cleaning up the dishes when the telephone rang. She grabbed the receiver expecting a call from her best girlfriend, Sherry. She flicked on the tape recorder, as she had been instructed to do, and answered the call. "Hello," she said.

A deep voice responded, "Is this Ashley?"

She hesitated at first but answered, "Yes. Who is this?"

"Who I am is not important, but give this message to your father. We could have taken Ruth Anne today. Maybe we will do it tomorrow, or next week. He knows what he needs to do for us."

Ashley listened intently and, without panicking, she said, "I'll tell him. If he does what you ask, will you leave us alone?"

"Yes, just tell him to keep his mouth shut. If he doesn't testify, no harm will come to your family."

"What about my father?"

"I can't say. He screwed up. If he helps us find the hit man, maybe things can be worked out."

"I can't call him, so you'll have to give me some time until he contacts me again."

"You better hope he calls again very soon," said the caller, abruptly ending their conversation.

Several moments elapsed before Ashley was able to calm herself down and stop shaking. She gulped the remains of her soda and slowly began to gain her composure. One of the cops assigned to the house was outside smoking a cigarette. She hurriedly looked and noticed he was still standing out on the patio. Quickly, she walked back to the recorder and erased the call. Her family was being threatened. She feared if the authorities knew about the call, they would not allow her to relay the message to her father, and she could not allow that to happen.

"I thought I heard the phone ringing. Did you just receive a call?" asked the officer, who was now standing behind her in the kitchen.

Somewhat startled, she said, "I didn't hear you come back in. You kind of scared me. Yes, I did receive a call from a friend of mine. She had some family stuff to talk about. I erased our conversation. I hope you don't mind, it was extremely personal."

"Well, I don't mind but the captain might. It's not proper procedure to erase any recording. Please don't do that again Mrs. Jenkins. I don't want either one of us to get in trouble. Okay?"

"Sorry, I did not intend to get you into trouble. I didn't realize it would be a problem. However, I'm sure my girlfriend will be very glad her personal business will remain confidential."

"We're okay, just so my boss doesn't find out. He wouldn't like it."

"I'm so sorry; I understand your predicament officer. I

can keep a secret if you can," she said, smiling innocently at him.

"Well, I'm sorry too, and I didn't mean to startle you Mrs. Jenkins."

* * *

Several days later, in a hotel suite not far from the Detroit Metropolitan Airport, Wallace, the star witness against mob boss Dominic Ricci, sat contemplating his probable fate. Ricci was charged with masterminding the plot against Stroh and his girlfriend. Whether Wallace testified or not, he had betrayed Ricci and knew he would be held accountable for his actions.

Wallace was not worried for himself but was fearful for his daughter's and granddaughter's safety. He figured Ashley's husband Peter, a former Marine, could take care of himself. Ricci was capable of getting retribution on anyone who crossed him, whether he was incarcerated or not. Wallace understood he would be looking over his shoulder for the rest of his life. He knew he was targeted for death now.

The police had told him that mobsters generally threaten retribution against the witness's family members, mostly prior to someone testifying against them. He was not surprised.

Inside the suite, Wallace opened the bedroom door, peered into the living room, and asked Sam Drake, his security officer, "Is it okay if I contact my daughter today? It's been about a week and I want to check and make sure she is alright."

Drake turned and said, "I'll need to get authorization first. You know it can be risky to make a call, even on a hotel phone. I'm sure they are fine. Besides, we would have heard otherwise if something had happened to them."

"I don't care. She is my only daughter and I'm very worried. I know what these mobsters are capable of doing."

"Yeah, we do too. That's why you and your family are being protected. Everything is going to be fine, you'll see. Once you give your testimony, and help put Ricci away, things will quiet down. The new boss will back away from you in time. His main emphasis will be on making money, not on retribution. He'll likely not want to mess with the police, regardless of what Ricci had previously arranged. Nevertheless, Ricci will probably put a contract on you."

"I'm sure he already has," said Wallace.

"Yeah, you are probably right. Why did you ever start working for him anyway?"

"It's a long story. Initially, my work was totally legitimate and my intention was to keep it that way. Over time some things changed, and eventually they became my largest client. I thought I could work for them and not be affected. I was too greedy and exercised poor judgment. You aren't recording this are you?"

"No, I was just curious," said Drake. "I'll call my boss

and see if you can make your call."

"Thanks, I appreciate it. By the way, I will deny everything I just told you in case I ever have to appear in court. It's my word against yours."

"Yeah, okay. I was just curious. I've heard you are a very smart lawyer."

Moments later, Wallace picked up the hotel phone and made his call.

The phone rang several times before Ashley answered it. "Hi, it's me," Wallace said. "How's your family?"

"So far we're alright. If you're able to talk without being overheard, I need to tell you something. I don't want the police to learn about this, so I've turned off the tape recorder."

"Yes, I'm alone. Go ahead," he said.

"I got a threatening call a couple of days ago. The caller said they could take Ruth Anne, whenever they wanted. The man said maybe they would do it tomorrow, or next week. It really scared me. You have no idea."

"What else did they say?"

"They told me to tell you to keep your mouth shut or else."

"What did you tell them?"

"I asked if our family would be safe, if you don't testify. The man said yes, but was unsure about you."

"I see."

"He said you screwed up, but maybe, if you help them find the hit man, they might reconsider."

"What do you want me to do?"

"Can those people be trusted to leave us alone, if you don't testify?"

"I don't know, but they're desperate. Regardless, I doubt if their offer would apply to me. I'm sorry I got you mixed up in this mess."

"Me too. What will happen to you if you don't testify?"

"Well, the Prosecutor has me on tape arranging for Stroh and his girlfriend to be murdered. They'd be able to use the information on the recording to implicate, prosecute, and convict me of several crimes."

"Dad, would you have to go to prison for a long time?"

"Yes, if I'm convicted, I'd have to do a lot of jail time."

"How much time would you get?"

"If I knew the charges, I could venture a guess. At least twenty years, I suppose. I'd say they'd charge me with accessory to attempted murder, plus the abduction charges for both Stroh and his girlfriend. Did the man tell you how to get in touch with them?"

"No Dad. All he said was for you to keep your mouth shut."

"I don't want anything bad to happen to you or your family. That's why I've decided I'm not going to testify."

"Are you sure? I don't want you to have to go to jail."

"Regardless, there is no way for me to win. If I testify against Ricci, I'm probably a dead man. If I don't testify against him, I'm betting he will probably back away from you and your family but not me. I am not willing to risk your safety anymore. I've got to go. I love you honey."

"I love you too Dad. Be careful and take care of yourself."

"I will. Talk to you later."

After the call ended, Wallace sat and contemplated his predicament.

I'm pretty much a dead man, whether I testify against Ricci or not. My doctor told me I have six months or so to live, considering that I have inoperable cancer.

All my troubles began, Wallace thought, *when I foolishly assured Ricci, several years ago, that I could convince State Senator Louis Stroh to support a Michigan state casino bill. The bill would have made it possible for the Family to be inconspicuously involved in a new casino being built in downtown Detroit. I was successful in gaining Stroh's support but he could not muster up enough votes to get the legislation passed on our timetable. Ricci was more than disappointed, he was furious. Not only had he given Stroh a generous amount of money for his help, but he had also, unbeknownst to Stroh, helped him end a terrible marriage by arranging for the accidental death of his wife.*

When it became apparent the senator would not be able to deliver the necessary votes for the casino legislation on time, we continued to seriously threaten him. Stroh's reaction to our warnings was to threaten us by indicating that he might go to the authorities, if we did not back down and give him more time. That's when Ricci decided we needed to hire a hit man to kill the senator and his girlfriend. In an effort to conceal the family's involvement in the crime, Ricci instructed his cousin, Tony Cavallaro, to eliminate the hit man too, once he had completed his work.

When Cavallaro failed to follow my instructions, and ended up ruining all of Ricci's plans, I was left with no other choice. I had to agree to testify against Ricci, in order to avoid prosecution, under the circumstance. And, as soon as Ricci found out about my deal to help the prosecutor, I am sure he immediately ordered my assassination.

Ricci was really naïve to think Cavallaro had the ability to get rid of the hit man for us. If only we had stuck to the original plan which did not include killing the hit man, Stroh and his girlfriend would now be dead and Ricci would be very relieved and satisfied with the results of the plan. Unfortunately, we didn't do it that way.

I am afraid for the lives of my family, but not my own. However, there is something I could do, in order to protect them from Ricci. Years ago, I contemplated the possibility of someday needing insurance, if Ricci ever turned against me. That is when I began to store duplicates of the major illegal activities from his family businesses, in my lockbox. If those documents ever surfaced, they could put him, and his associates, away for a long time and ruin their businesses. If I held those documents over his head, it might be possible to maintain enough leverage against him to protect us all, at least for a while.

Why the hell did I ever get myself into this mess anyway? Greed, I guess. Ricci paid me really well for all those years. But, if I had never worked for Ricci, my family undoubtedly would not be in jeopardy now.

Several minutes elapsed before Wallace picked up the phone again and called Ricci's private number. The phone rang and the familiar voice of Minello answered, "Military Surplus Depot."

"Paul, this is Wallace calling."

"Yeah, I know."

"Tell Ricci I got his message and I have decided not to testify against him. However, I want his assurances that my family will never be harmed. If he agrees, I will help him find the hit man too. I have the guy's voice on tape."

"I'll tell him," said Minello.

"Also, tell Dominic I am not the only one to blame for the indictment levied against him. I've heard the hit man made a tape recording of one of our conversations and he must have given it to the authorities. I had nothing to do with the recording. He must have done it on his own"

"Okay," Minello said,

"Paul, you know that Tony never really listens to anyone," said Wallace. "If he weren't related to Dominic, he'd have been finished a long time ago. He should have followed my advice and stayed farther away from the hit man than he did. If he'd done as I suggested things probably would have ended up much differently. And, this indictment against Dominic might never have occurred. I hope Dominic realizes his cousin Tony, at the very least, is more than partially to blame for this mess. I'll contact you again," said Wallace, as he ended the call.

Chapter 5

Tony Cavallaro was in his favorite recliner watching a Tigers baseball game, enjoying beer and pizza, when the telephone rang. He cursed at the interruption, and reluctantly got up to answer the phone. "Hello," he said.

"Dominic wants to see you right away," barked Minello.

"What's up? We're playing the Yanks and Higginson just got a home run! What a ballgame," he said.

"Hey, get your ass in gear and quit fucking around," said Minello. "He'll meet you at the surplus store in half-an-hour. Just be there."

"Sure, see you in thirty minutes. Ask Dominic if he wants beer or something."

"Just get going," snapped the man.

Cavallaro was a made guy and an occasional family enforcer. He didn't appreciate the disrespect and short tone Minello displayed.

I hate that little son-of-a-bitch, thought Cavallaro. I would like to knock the shit out of him. What an asshole.

But, within a few minutes, Tony was out the door and driving toward Ricci's office, located just off the Interstate. Despite the heavy traffic, Cavallaro arrived right on time. A neon sign, identifying the Military Surplus Depot, was conspicuously posted across the front of the building.

He parked the dirty, late model Cadillac in a spot on the right side of the building. Cavallaro's priorities did not include keeping his vehicle clean. As he exited the car, he noticed his back seat was full of trash, and made a mental note to give the car a good cleaning.

Cavallaro opened the front door and entered the business. There were only a few customers inside. The store had countless racks of military clothing, supplies, and war-time artifacts in numerous display cases.

He walked back towards the rear of the store to the door marked "Private". Upon entering the room, he noticed Minello, Ricci's underboss, standing next to his cousin Dominic, who was seated at a mahogany desk. Looking up to meet Cavallaro's eye, Ricci motioned for him to sit down in the wooden chair in front of the desk.

"It's about time you showed. We were wondering if you were coming. Why were you late?"

"Fuck you Paulie, I'm on time. What's up Dominic?" Tony asked.

"Don't be so sensitive Tony, I was just busting your balls for fun," said Minello.

"Cut the crap you two," said Ricci. "I want to tell you some good news. We finally were able to talk to Wallace's daughter. We threatened her and told her to relay our warning to her Dad. Paul told her to tell him, he'd better keep his mouth shut or else something bad would happen to his grandchild."

"Okay," said Cavallaro, wondering if this was the only reason he had been sent for today.

"Two days after Paul talked with the daughter; Wallace called us back to say he would not be testifying against me, as long as I would guarantee his family's safety. Paul assured him that I would guarantee it."

"You aren't actually going to follow through with that guarantee are you?" asked Cavallaro.

"Hell no, but he doesn't need to know that. He asked, if he helped us find the hit man, would we give him a pass," said Ricci.

"What did you say?"

"I didn't respond," Minello interjected. "I recommend we give him a temporary pass but not forever. Maybe just long enough to fake an accidental death or something."

"What do you want me to do Dominic?" asked Cavallaro.

"He said he saw the hit man and has a recording of his voice. He claims he can identify the guy and help us find him. You saw him and heard his voice too, right?"

"Yeah, but I'm sure he was disguised."

"Could you identify him?"

"I don't know Dominic. I only saw him twice. The first time, I can't say whether he was disguised or not. He looked like a queer to me, dressed in running gear and the other stuff. I didn't pay much attention to him. The second time, he covered my face and it was at night. I'd like to meet him again though, and repay him for cutting off my finger."

"Don't worry, you'll get your chance," said Ricci.

"I wonder what Wallace plans to tell the authorities, if he doesn't testify against you," said Minello. "Whatever he tells them, I guarantee they will be pissed."

"He might use the attorney/client legal provision," said Ricci.

"Never heard of it, but I don't think he'd risk fucking you over again Dominic. He'll probably work with us since we threatened his grandkid," said Minello.

"I don't trust Wallace, and as soon as we have identified and located the hit man too, I want them both brought back here alive," said Ricci. "Understand?"

"I'll happily take care of it," said Cavallaro. "You need anything else?"

"One more thing, Paul will be the one giving you instructions before you do anything else. Okay?"

"Yeah, alright."

"Sorry to disturb your game but this couldn't wait," Minello said, sarcastically.

"It's not a problem. Call me any time."

* * *

Back at the hotel, Wallace was still contemplating his options. He had very few, if he wanted to ensure the safety of his family. However, his own prospects looked bleak at best, even if he helped Ricci find the hit man.

I wonder if I can really trust Ricci to keep his word, regarding the safety of my family. Dominic is a ruthless mobster but I've never heard of him going back on his word. He did, however, note the lack of response from Minello on the question of his fate. Not a good sign. I wonder if the old adage, "there is no honor amongst thieves" applies in my case. I will probably have to accept the consequences for my actions, in order to protect my family. But, I might still have a slight chance to work things out. I guess I will have to wait and see, he thought.

Wallace got up from the chair and opened the door to the living room. Drake, one of the assigned security men, looked up at him when he entered the room.

"What's up Wallace, you hungry again?"

"No, I need to talk with your boss. I've decided I'm not going to testify."

"Are you crazy?" said Drake. "You'll be a dead man, along with your family, if you don't testify. How did Ricci get to you?"

"I'm a dead man anyway. Hey, I know my rights a lot better than you. Call your boss and arrange a meeting. I'm sure she will want to talk to me."

"You won't have a chance whether you beat the charges or not. Ricci can get to you on the outside, as well as in prison. You know that, right?"

"There's nothing more to talk about. I've made up my mind!"

"Okay, I'll call her."

Is she ever going to be upset, thought Drake!

"You might as well go back in the bedroom until I talk with her Wallace. You may want to rethink your decision before she gets here."

"Fine, let me know when she arrives."

* * *

Amanda Jefferson was the Wayne County Deputy Prosecutor in charge of the Ricci case. Her office had been trying for years to pin something on Ricci and the Detroit Partnership. Unfortunately, she had been unsuccessful in her prior attempts. During the time Wallace was Ricci's attorney, he made sure the family stayed as far away from the grips of the law as possible. Jefferson had only met Wallace a few times, but she knew of his exceptional skills and reputation. Few lawyers possessed the legal astuteness that Wallace did, and she was shocked when he was implicated in the Stroh kidnapping/conspiracy to commit murder plot.

When her private telephone line rang, she picked up the receiver and said, "Amanda Jefferson."

"Ms. Jefferson, this is Sam Drake, the security officer assigned to Henry Wallace. He wanted me to tell you that he's decided not to testify."

There was a short silence on the line and then Jefferson spoke, "What in the world? How could that have happened? Did someone call him or something? "

"As far as I know, today was the only time he has used the hotel phone, and that was to call his daughter."

"Besides for today, has he made, or received, any other calls?"

"Yes, he called his daughter last weekend too."

"What in the hell could have happened? I don't believe this shit. That son-of-a-bitch Wallace!"

"What do you want me to do?"

"Bring him to the jail. I need to see him right away. Maybe I can get him to change his mind. His family is alright, aren't they?"

"Yes, as far as I know."

"If Wallace doesn't testify against Ricci, he'll probably be killed immediately. He needs to know this stunt will probably end disastrously for him," said Jefferson.

"I agree. When do you want him at the jail?"

"You can bring him now. I'll be waiting for him in the lawyer's conference room on the third floor."

"Okay, I'll see you in about thirty minutes," said Drake.

"Be careful," warned Jefferson.

"Thank you, I will," he said.

* * *

Ten minutes later, the phone rang at the Military Surplus store. "Is Ricci there?"

"Not right now, but I can take a message."

"This is Sheriff Jones. Tell my friend they are bringing Wallace to the main jail in about thirty minutes. Ask him if he wants me to do anything."

"Just a minute, he just walked in," said Minello. "Your friend says thanks but nothing now."

* * *

The basement entrance to the main jail, on Clinton Street in downtown Detroit, is protected by security cameras and a 10-foot, barbed-wire, chain-link fence. When a vehicle approaches the entrance, a guard verifies the occupants inside, before the mechanical gate is opened. Once the vehicle is inside, the gate closes and an overhead door leading down a ramped entrance is opened.

Right on time, Drake appeared at the chain-link gate, driving a black unmarked cruiser. In the back seat of the vehicle were Wallace, and John Flanders, another security officer. The vehicle entered through the gate and disappeared down the ramp to the basement. The two men emerged with Wallace and were immediately greeted by several Sheriff's deputies, who escorted the men to the elevators.

The third floor of the jail was filled with interrogation rooms and one lawyer's conference room. Inside the conference room Deputy Prosecutor Jefferson waited.

When Wallace appeared in the room, Jefferson immediately takes charge. "Put the witness in that chair," she said, pointing to the wooden chair farthest away from the window.

"Madame Deputy Prosecutor, it's a pleasure," Wallace said, as he extended his hand.

Jefferson looked directly at Wallace, ignored his gesture, and said, "I heard you've had a change of heart. We need to talk."

"Okay let's talk," said Wallace.

"Before we do, Drake, will you and your partner leave us alone for a few minutes?"

"Sure, we'll be right outside if you need us," Drake said.

"Mr. Wallace, do you know you are about to be killed

and your family too?" said Jefferson.

"I know there are risks either way," Wallace said.

"Before we talk about the risks, what happened to make you change your mind about testifying?"

"I just decided today to change my mind and invoke the attorney/client privilege provision, as is my right under statute to do."

"Well, it may be your right but you will be found guilty of several crimes and go to prison for a very long time, where you will probably either die of old age or be killed by Ricci. Is that alright with you?"

"Life is risky."

"What about your family? Have you considered their fate?"

"Yes."

"How did they get to you?"

"I have no idea what you're talking about."

"You know we have a tape recording with your voice on it, talking to a hit man about killing Senator Stroh and his girlfriend. It's obvious you made the arrangements for Ricci."

"No, I didn't!"

"We have a statement from the Senator and his girlfriend, confirming that someone had kidnapped them and was originally intending to kill them. The Senator told us that you were representing Ricci when you met with him in Holland."

"Can you prove that?"

"Yes I can. Do you realize, if you don't testify, we will have no other choice than to pull off the security team for your family? Is that alright with you?"

"You have to do what you think is right Madame Prosecutor."

"Regardless of what I think, you've given me no other choice. The rules on witness protection are pretty clear. If you don't testify, you, and your family, lose the security detail."

"Okay."

"Is that what you're going to say when I tell you someone kidnapped your daughter or granddaughter and killed them?"

After Jefferson's comment, Wallace became quiet and failed to offer a response to her question.

Reacting to his obvious concern, Jefferson asked, "Is this what you really want to do? We can protect you and your family but only if you cooperate! Once you testify, we can arrange to relocate everybody and you'll never have to worry about Ricci again. You think about it tonight. I'm keeping you in jail for your protection, and I'll see you in the morning. Do you have anything else to say?"

Wallace paused for a moment and said, "I'm not going to testify. Besides, I'm innocent. I'll take my chances in a court of law."

"Okay, I'm going to pull your family's security detail in a day or two, and I'm going to ask the judge to keep you in jail, at least until you've been charged. You may want to reconsider your decision before it's too late. You will be formally charged with accessory to kidnapping and attempted murder within forty-eight hours. I'm going to request that you be denied bail. Good luck to you sir," said Jefferson with a long, cold stare.

Wallace stared confidently back at her and said with a self-assured smile, "I'll see you in court Madame Prosecutor."

Chapter 6

Bartlett arrived at the Ursula Shop promptly at nine, with a cup of coffee and a copy of the local newspaper. Rosa was busy cleaning the display cases as he entered. "Morning," she said.

"Good morning Rosa. How was your weekend?"

"Really good. My girlfriends and I got together Saturday night, and we partied until early Sunday morning," she said, beaming.

"I hope things didn't get too wild and crazy," said Bartlett. "I've heard stories about you Island girls!"

"Oh Mr. Bartlett, you're too funny. You know better than that, we are all good girls."

"Yeah, I know. I was just teasing you. Were there many men at the party? You told me several weeks ago that you felt lonely sometimes."

"Several guys stopped by but I am not interested in any of them. I haven't been with a man since my husband. However, I have thought about it," she said.

"Well, I'm certain that eventually you'll find somebody you like."

"Yeah, maybe someday," Rosa said with a sigh.

Maybe I already have found somebody, she thought to herself.

"I need to work in my office for a while," Bartlett said, "I'd rather not be disturbed."

"No problem Mr. Bartlett, I can handle everything."

I'll bet you can, he thought. She looked unusually sexy and happy for a Monday morning. He fantasized about her voluptuous body hidden under her colorful cotton dress. Too bad I'll never get to see it. It's hard to believe she's still alone.

Several hours later, Bartlett emerged from his office and announced to Rosa, "I need to go out of town for a week or so. Can you take care of the shop while I'm gone?"

"You're going back to the Mainland again Mr. Bartlett?"

"Unfortunately, I am. There are several things I need to do, but I'll be back before you know it."

"Alright, I'll keep things running here," she said, trying not to look too disappointed concerning his absence.

* * *

As he walked to the baggage claim area, Bartlett thought O'Hare seemed unusually busy for a Tuesday afternoon. He planned for a short visit with Moira to help her prepare for the move to St. Croix. The couple had been talking about his trip for the past several weeks. Moira told him to expect lots of packing and chaos if she decided to move.

Unbeknownst to Bartlett, Moira had contacted a local realtor for an appraisal of her home. She planned to put her house on the market once their wedding plans had been finalized. Pauline had offered to store some of her more expensive furniture indefinitely in her basement. Due to the high cost of shipping to the Virgin Islands, Moira decided to sell her unwanted things and take only a small amount of personal items and clothing to St. Croix. They had previously agreed she would not leave Evanston, or quit her job, until after her home had been sold.

Also, Bartlett had another reason to return to Chicago. He wanted to retrieve the last of his cash, from a small Savings and Loan safety deposit box, and move it to St. Croix. Bartlett planned to buy plenty of merchandise to resell, enclose the cash with the merchandise, and ship it back to the Ursula Shop.

Upon arriving in the baggage claim area, Bartlett quickly retrieved his bag and proceeded through the lower-level doors to the cab stand, where he hailed the nearest taxi. The red-headed, cheeky, overweight driver placed his luggage in the trunk and diligently got back into the cab. "Where to buddy?" he asked.

"Evanston, near Ridge Avenue and Dempster."

"You got the address?" asked the cabbie.

"Of course, take 90 E. It should take about thirty minutes to get there depending on traffic," Bartlett said.

The cab shot off like a race car at the Indianapolis 500. "What's the hurry buddy?" Bartlett asked.

"See what time it is?"

"Yes."

"Well, in thirty minutes 90E will be backed up so bad it will take Ex-Lax to get us through it. Trust me I know what I'm talking about," said the impatient cab driver.

"Yeah, I used to live here too, but I've forgotten how hectic rush hour traffic can be."

"Where'd you live?"

"Over on the south side. I grew up there, but it's been a long time since I've been back."

"What brings you to Chicago?" asked the cabbie, inquisitively.

"I have a girlfriend who lives here and we're getting married," said Bartlett, happily.

"Good luck. I tried it once, but things didn't work out so well. Didn't want to be married to a cheater. Several months after getting married, I decided to surprise her and take a half day off from work. Caught the bitch in bed with another man."

"What did you do to them?" asked Bartlett.

"Nothing, I was so pissed off I moved out that day. Never regretted it," the cabbie said. "Lucky because we didn't have kids."

"This is my first time."

"Congratulations, hope you have better luck than I did."

"Thanks," said Bartlett.

I hope so too, he thought.

About thirty minutes later, Bartlett directed the driver to within several blocks of Moira's house. He took his bag and gave the cabbie a good tip. "Be safe," Bartlett told the man.

"Sure will. Thanks for the tip," the driver said, as he pulled away from the curb.

Bartlett walked to Moira's back door, retrieved the spare key, and entered the house. It was just after three, and he knew she probably wouldn't be home until five. He put his suitcase in the bedroom and decided to take a quick shower to freshen up before dinner.

* * *

Wednesday morning, inside the Wayne County jail, Wallace awakened early and got up to use the toilet. He had spent another restless night in jail and wondered what this day would bring. Hungry and tired, he was hopeful he would not have to eat too many more jailhouse meals.

Sammie Parker, his attorney, finally assured him that he would be allowed to post bond and go home. They were waiting on the Deputy Prosecutor and a Judge to come to an agreement concerning bail before allowing his release.

A trustee delivered chipped beef on toast for breakfast in the usual, dented metal tray. "Thanks, but it looks like dog food," he told the guy with a disgusted look on his face.

"Yeah, it don't taste too bad though," said the thin, sickly-looking, black man, wearing an orange trustee uniform. "Best you get used to it cause it don't get no better. Most times it be worse. You'll eat it if you is hungry enough."

"I'm glad to say I won't. I should be getting bailed out of here today," Wallace said.

"You one lucky mother-fucker. Hell, I ain't never had money for bond. What they got you for?"

"Accessory to kidnapping and attempted murder, but I'm innocent."

"Sure as shit, and you say you is getting out? You must've gotten you a good lawyer," the trustee said with a doubtful look on his face.

"I am a lawyer."

The trustee just shook his head, said nothing, and left feeling resentful. As he pushed the delivery cart towards the next cell, Wallace could hear him faintly say, "Them mother-fucking crackers get all the breaks."

Several hours later, two large guards arrived and informed Wallace they would be transporting him to court for his formal hearing on bail. Wallace was led to a private room inside the courthouse where he awaited his attorney.

"How do you like Wayne County's accommodations Henry?" Samantha asked, upon entering the room.

"I've had much better."

"I'm sure," she said. "I met with the Deputy Prosecutor and she reluctantly agreed to set bail at one million dollars. They don't consider you a flight risk, but they are worried you will be killed once you're released. Are you worried?"

"Sure, under the circumstances I am, but I think Ricci will keep me alive for a while. I have information he wants and for other reasons too."

"What reasons?"

"I'd rather not say right now but, if anything happens to me, there are some specific instructions for you in a manila envelope in my desk drawer at home."

"Is there anything more you need from me?"

"No, just keep me posted. Thanks, I owe you one," Wallace stated.

* * *

Early afternoon, a jail officer arrived at Wallace's cell informing him that his bond had been posted and he would be getting out of jail fairly soon. Upon his release, Wallace hailed a cab in front of the jail and headed for a favorite restaurant in Gross Pointe, for a late lunch. An hour later he returned home and proceeded to his office where he retrieved a .45-caliber pistol from a desk drawer. Sitting down behind his desk, he proceeded to call Ricci. The phone rang several times before Minello finally answered.

"I need to talk to Dominic," said Wallace. "Would you get him on the phone?"

"Are you recording this call Henry?" questioned Dominic, when he got on the phone.

"No. Why do you ask?"

"Because you're a very clever man," said Ricci.

"Thanks, I'm certain that's why you hired me."

"How was jail? I heard they released you this afternoon."

"Their accommodations are not the best. I wouldn't recommend them. You know, you should thank me for keeping you out of the Wayne County Jail and more than once," said Wallace.

"Maybe but let's not talk about it now. Tell me everything you know about the hit man, how you made your tape recording, etc."

"Well, you recommended him. I got his name from the list you provided. He was from Chicago and I contacted him through a company called JBS Consulting. His office was in the Kenilworth building in the Loop. I spoke in person to a strange little character by the name of Franklin D. Russo who presumably worked, in some capacity, for him."

"Go on," said Ricci.

"Initially, I wired an upfront down payment to his Cayman banking account. After he assured me, and offered proof, that he had killed Stroh and the girl, I paid the remaining balance to him with cash. I can get you the wiring information from my brokerage firm later this afternoon, or in the morning."

"What proof did he provide?"

"He gave me a bloody finger with Stroh's ring on it. I assumed the finger belonged to Stroh."

"I see. What did you do with the ring and the finger?" Ricci asked.

"I got rid of them," said Wallace.

"Did you use Family funds to pay the hit man?"

"No, I used my own money. I figured you'd reimburse me."

"If things would have worked out differently I would have. Anyway, go on," said Ricci.

"I recorded his voice several times, although I wonder if he had disguised it somehow. I'll send the tapes to you but I have to go to the office to get them."

"Where and when did you see him?"

"I saw him only once after he called to tell me the job

had been completed. We arranged to meet at the Holiday Inn near Toledo, right off the Interstate. He is about six feet tall, and I believe he was wearing a wig. The hit man had a fake looking, short, dark-colored beard and appeared to be very muscular. He was well-spoken, very poised, decisive, and unemotional. The guy was all business. He seemed to be someone you would not want to mess with. Initially, I warned Tony about him, but he didn't listen to me."

"Okay. Is there anything else?"

"Yes, I am expecting you to keep your word concerning my family's safety. Can I trust you?"

"My word is always good. If you hold up your end of the deal there will be no problems."

"I will. Incidentally, I forgot to tell you the other day that I have some very interesting files on you and the family businesses stored away for safe-keeping. We understand each other, don't we?"

After a brief pause Ricci responded, "I'm a man of my word Henry, but don't ever threaten me again. Just keep your fucking mouth shut, help us find the contractor, and everything will be fine. Understand?"

"Yes."

"I'll be in touch," Ricci said, as he slammed the receiver down. "Fuck," he said to Minello. "I'm going to kill that fucking lawyer, and maybe his entire family too, when this is done!"

Chapter 7

Bartlett returned to Moira's house around four Wednesday afternoon. The trunk of her car was crammed with merchandise that he had purchased for resale in the shop. Contained in his briefcase was the cash from the Savings and Loan. After he backed the car into the garage, he put his purchases on top of the work bench. It took him forty-five minutes to pack the merchandise into four cartons and prepare them for shipping. After placing the cash into one of the cartons, Bartlett put all four cartons into the trunk, locked the car, the garage door, and went back to the house. He planned to have the boxes shipped the following morning.

Bartlett looked at his watch. It was almost five o'clock and he knew Moira would be coming home soon. They had planned to have an early dinner at a local Mexican restaurant and then go see a movie.

Swordfish, Hannibal, and Blow were all being shown at the James Theatre in Evanston. They decided on Swordfish. Moira liked John Travolta and Hugh Jackman, and Bartlett wanted to see Halle Berry. He was specifically intrigued by the Swordfish plot, which involved Travolta as a renegade counter-terrorist, attempting to steal billions of United States government dirty money.

When I stole dirty money from a drug dealer in New Orleans a couple of years ago, my activities, compared to the Swordfish plot, would only be worthy of a footnote instead of a movie. If only I had planned to steal the drug dealer's money in the beginning, I would have had more to show for my efforts, thought Bartlett. At one point, I could have stolen almost a million dollars.

Earlier in the day, he had read the Tribune's movie review about Swordfish and the other films. The thought of seeing Halle Berry's naked body excited him, but he decided not to mention it to Moira.

At the conclusion of the movie, Moira asked, "What did you think of Halle Berry?"

"She's alright," he said.

"You're such a liar," Moira said, slapping him on the shoulder and laughing. "It's okay to look, just don't touch," she said. "She is gorgeous."

"Yes she is," he said, grinning. "But, you said it, not me. I'm just agreeing with you."

Next door to the theater was an ice cream parlor where they shared a hot fudge sundae. Afterwards, they went home and got into bed.

"If it's alright with you, I don't feel like making love tonight," said Moira. "Between the buttered popcorn and the hot fudge sundae, my stomach is kind of upset."

"It's fine," said Bartlett. "Hope you feel better in the morning."

"I hope so too," she said, giving him a goodnight kiss.

The next day they arose early and Moira was off to work. Around noon, Bartlett dropped off the cartons to be shipped. He declared the contents in the cartons as merchandise for resale in his business.

* * *

In Detroit, several blocks from 9-mile road, Cavallaro stopped at a self-serve car wash to detail his car. Previously, Tony had stopped there to wash his Cadillac before heading downtown. It had been more than a month since he had bothered cleaning his car and it was filthy again.

He pulled the two-door Eldorado into the parking lot and stopped at the vacuum machine units to sweep the car. Cavallaro got out, pushed the front seat forward, and reached into the back seat to gather the accumulated trash scattered on the seats, and the floor.

Normally he would look at the debris as he worked to see if it needed to be kept or discarded. A small yellow laundry tag briefly caught his attention. He shoved it into his hand with the other pieces of trash he had retrieved. When he squeezed his fist to compress the contents, he felt a sharp prick in the palm of his hand. He quickly opened his hand and discovered the yellow tag had a straight pin sticking through it. Inquisitively, he opened the tag and saw the words, "Wong Cleaners, Evanston, IL" printed in small type on one side of the tag.

How in the hell would I get a laundry tag from Illinois in the back seat of my car, he wondered.

He pulled the pin out, discarding it, and the rest of the debris, into a nearby waste container. Cavallaro unrolled the vacuum hose from its holder and started sweeping the floor. Suddenly, he stopped and thought about the tag again. He reached into the trash barrel, retrieved the tag, and again wondered how it had gotten into his car.

No one ever rides in the back seat of my car and I haven't been to Illinois for over a year. Come to think of it, the only person who rode in my back seat lately was the hit man who cut off my finger. I wonder if the tag dropped out of his pocket on the way to the Dune Buggy place, where he left me in Saugatuck, Michigan. Maybe the motherfucker lives in Evanston. I need to check this out right away. If I can find out whether or not the tag belonged to him, maybe Dominic will forgive me for screwing up the Stroh hit in Saugatuck.

* * *

Mid-morning on Thursday, Ricci was reading the business section of the Detroit Free Press when the telephone rang in his office. Minello answered the call.

"Paulie, this is Tony. I need to speak with Dominic right away."

"I'll see if he is available," said Minello. He covered the phone and said to Ricci, "It's Tony calling, and he wants to talk to you."

"What does he want?" asked Ricci, curiously.

"He sounds excited about something."

"Okay, I'll talk to him," Ricci said, grabbing the receiver from Minello and saying, "What do you need, Tony?"

"Dominic, I was cleaning my car and found something in the back seat. I think it belonged to the guy who cut off my finger. He's the only person who's been in my back seat for months."

"Really, what is it?"

"It's a laundry tag from Evanston, Illinois."

"Does it have a name on it?"

"Yes, Wong Cleaners."

"Bring it to me right away. I want to see it," Ricci said.

"I'll be there after I've finished washing my car."

"Okay, but hurry up."

Ricci turned to Minello and said, "Paul, get me a road map of Illinois. I think there's one in the pocket behind the driver's seat in my car. Tony may have stumbled onto a lead for our hit man."

"I'll get it right away," Minello said.

* * *

Forty-five minutes later, Tony arrived at the surplus store. He walked back to Ricci's office and entered the room. He was holding a small yellow tag in his hand. "Here is the tag I was telling you about Dominic."

"Let me see it," Ricci said, grabbing it out of his hand. He looked at the tag and read the name of Wong Cleaners, Evanston, Illinois on one side. "If this tag belonged to the hit man, how could it have gotten into your back seat?" inquired Ricci.

"Only thing I can figure is it must have fallen out of his pocket. He was wearing a light-weight jacket. No one else has been in my back seat for months and I haven't been to Illinois in over a year. I don't think I've ever been to Evanston. In fact, I don't even know where it is," said Cavallaro.

"Are you positive?"

"Yeah."

"Okay, good work. Here's what I want you to do. The tag has a number on the other side of it. I want you to drive to Evanston, locate the business, and see if you can get the name and address of the person corresponding to the number. If you get the information, call me and I'll give you further instructions. Do not try to investigate anything further until after you have talked to me. Understand?"

"Yes, when I find something out I'll call you right away."

"I want you to leave for Chicago today. Evanston is north of the city. Go home and pack a bag. You might have to stay for several days. Try not to screw things up this time Tony. We will be very lucky if we get another chance to find him."

"I'll do my best. I want this guy as bad as you do Dominic, maybe worse."

"Listen to me very carefully Tony. Do exactly as I tell you to do. Understand?"

"Yeah, sure I will Dominic. But if I'm lucky enough to find the guy, he's dead," said Cavallaro.

"No, first I want you to bring him to me. I want to talk to him before you kill him." Turning to Minello, Ricci said, "Paul, I want you to send somebody reliable with Tony, just in case he needs help."

"Dominic, I can handle it," stated Cavallaro.

"Yeah, I know you can, but I want to make sure this time."

"I don't think it's necessary to …"

Ricci interrupted him and said, "Just do as you're told. Check with Paul before you leave for Evanston. You'll need to pick up his guy before you take off."

"Okay Dominic!"

"Just do your work and don't fuck it up. Understand?"

"Yes Dominic!"

* * *

Back in Evanston, Bartlett had spent an uneventful day at Moira's house. There was a Cubs ballgame on television, and he had spent most of the afternoon watching it between several naps.

Moira had thawed out some rib-eye steaks for dinner. He expected to have their long awaited talk about his proposal after the meal. Based on several of their earlier conversations, Bartlett believed Moira had already decided to get married and move to St. Croix. He was hopeful she would make it official tonight.

Moira arrived home at the usual time. She hurried to the kitchen to prepare dinner. Bartlett walked up behind her while she was standing at the sink, put his hands on her waist, and said, "Are you too busy to say hello?"

She turned quickly and said, "You startled me. I thought you were asleep, and I didn't want to disturb you. How was your day?"

"Not bad. Actually, it was great, just not the usual for me."

"I thought St. Croix was such a relaxing place?"

"Oh it is, I just have more work to do there."

"Once we start packing, you are going to wish you were back on the island."

"Sounds like you've made up your mind."

"Yes, I have. I've known for a while. Are you happy?"

"I am," he said, as he gave her a nice kiss and a hug.

"There's only one condition, which I insist you must agree to before I can make it official."

"What's that," asked Bartlett.

"You have to promise me you will never work for the United States government again. If you can't, we won't be getting married, and I won't be moving to St. Croix."

"I'm done," he promised. "I'll never work for them again. Do you have any champagne?"

"Why do we need champagne?"

"For the celebration, of course," Bartlett said.

"I have a better idea."

"Really, what's your idea?"

"Let's have a nice meal, take a short walk, and get comfortable for the evening. How's that sound?"

"It sounds perfect, but how is your stomach doing?" Bartlett asked, placing his hand on her tummy.

"I am feeling just fine tonight," she said, smiling brightly at him.

Chapter 8

Early Friday morning, Bartlett got up to use the bathroom. When he got back into bed, Moira was reading a book. "I couldn't sleep," she said. "If the light bothers you, I'll turn it off."

"Its fine," said Bartlett. "I'm having trouble sleeping too. What's wrong with us?"

"I guess we went to bed too early."

"I guess so," said Bartlett. "Moira, I have something I need to tell you about myself before we get married," he said, nervously.

"What is it?"

"Well … I know you are aware that I worked for the United States Government, but I never told you in what department. I worked for the Central Intelligence Agency."

"I'm not surprised," she said. "You once told me you were doing something secretive for the government, so I always assumed you worked for one of the intelligence agencies. But, up until now, I didn't know for sure."

"That's right, I did tell you. Anyway, when you work for the CIA or the Agency as they call it, you can be reactivated at any time."

"What! Are you kidding me?" she said.

"Unfortunately, I'm not kidding. However, the Agency assured me I will not have to worry about reactivation due to my age. I'd like to believe them, but you never know."

"So ... what are you saying?"

"Last evening, I told you as far as I'm concerned, my work for the United States Government is over and it is. However, there is always a small chance they might contact me for another assignment, which is why I want to be totally honest with you, because that's how it works in the CIA."

"What am I supposed to do? You know how I feel," said Moira.

"Yes, I do. However, I have one important advantage over most of the former agents. They don't know where I live. Therefore, it will be much harder for them to reactivate me. I've been using one of those local box office businesses to forward my mail to St. Croix. Have you told anyone I live in St. Croix?"

"Only my girlfriend, Pauline."

"Are you certain? Maybe you've forgotten and have told someone else, perhaps at work?"

"Pauline is the only person I've told. I have always made it a practice to keep my business and personal life separate. My boss and a few co-workers know I am vacationing with you somewhere in the Caribbean, but I never specified where."

"Does anyone besides Pauline know my name?"

"No, whenever I have talked about you, I have either referred to you as my boyfriend or Jim. I've never used your last name."

"Okay. How many people do you think Pauline has told?"

"I'd say none, but I'll check with her later today. As my best friend, I would assume she hasn't told anyone about my personal business. Besides, she doesn't have many other friends or acquaintances. I'm pretty sure she feels the same as me about keeping her personal life private. If Pauline tells me she hasn't told anyone your name or address, I'd believe her."

"Well, I hope you're right."

"Jimmy, Pauline is from a small town near Milwaukee, Wisconsin. I personally know she hasn't established many friendships since she's been in Illinois. She's kind of a loner like I was before we met."

"What about your relatives?"

"You know they are mostly elderly and I haven't seen or heard from them in years. Heck, my mother doesn't even know anything about you other than how we met."

"Alright, good," said Bartlett, sounding relieved.

"You worry too much Jimmy. I'll quiz Pauline this

evening. I'd be very surprised if you have anything to worry about from her."

"I certainly hope not. I cautioned you about discussing my life for security reasons. Now you know why!"

"Jimmy, Pauline only knows you live in St. Croix and that your name is Jim Bartlett. She has no idea you work for the Government or what you've done in the past. After all, I didn't know myself until now. Pauline is my best friend. It would have been almost impossible for me to share nothing with her concerning you."

"I'm sorry honey. I agree you're right. But, if I seem paranoid about my personal business, it's because I need to be extra careful. I hope you understand," said Bartlett. "I'm just concerned about our safety. I've made some very nasty enemies in my line of work with the CIA."

"I understand."

"Does Pauline still live in the gray and white house?"

"Yes. Don't you remember? It's over on Payne Street where I showed you."

"Oh yes, now I remember. It's been a while since I've been by there."

"Why are you asking about where Pauline lives?"

"Well, you never know, I might need to meet you there sometime."

"Oh alright," she said. "Let's try to go back to sleep. Okay?"

"Alright," he said.

John W. Gemmer

* * *

It was early Friday morning when Cavallaro awoke and reached for his cigarettes. He and Jimmy Parisi had arrived in Evanston late Thursday evening. They stopped at a local bar for a beer and a sandwich before checking into the motel. They planned to get up around seven o'clock, eat breakfast, and look for Wong Cleaners.

Cavallaro was not too happy about being accompanied by Parisi, but he also was not prepared to tell his cousin, or Minello, to go screw themselves either. Cousin or not, he was sure Dominic was still angry with him for the screw-ups in Saugatuck.

At six-thirty he got up, called Parisi, and took a shower. A half-hour later they met for breakfast at the greasy spoon next to the motel. Cavallaro waved at Parisi as he walked into the cafe. "Over here," he said. "I have a fresh pot of coffee."

Parisi poured a cup for himself and casually announced, "This job isn't going to be too hard."

"What do you mean?"

"Well, I checked the phone book last night before going to bed. According to the yellow pages, Wong Cleaners is located on the corner of Church and Wesley Avenue near downtown."

"Yeah, I checked the phone book too," said Cavallaro.

"I figure we are a couple miles away," Parisi said.

"After breakfast, we'll drive over to the cleaners and ask about the tag."

"I can use my police badge to help us get information."

"Really, you've got a police officer's shield? Where'd you get it?"

"Dominic is friends with somebody on the police force. I've used the badge before to get out of speeding tickets."

"That's handy," said Parisi.

"Yeah, I'll flash it at Wong's. Most people see the badge and cooperate immediately without any hassles. Maybe we'll get lucky."

"Sounds good, but I've never done it before," said Parisi.

"You'll see what I mean, it's really easy. Trust me."

* * *

It took about ten minutes for Cavallaro and Parisi to find the cleaners. Cavallaro parked the car in front of the store. "Look serious," Cavallaro said to Parisi, when they got out of the car. "I'll do all the talking. Just try to look official."

Parisi opened the front door setting off a small bell that chimed announcing their arrival. Within moments an attractive, young, oriental woman appeared at the counter. "May I help you?" she asked.

Trying to appear official, Cavallaro responded, "I'm Officer Anthony," quickly flashing his badge and returning it to his pocket. "I need to ask you a few questions."

"What is this about?"

"We're investigating a felony." He pulled out the yellow laundry tag and asked, "Is this your tag?"

"Can I see it please?" she asked, as she held out her hand.

"Sure," said Cavallaro, as he handed it to her. "Do you recognize it?"

"Yes," the woman nodded, "it is ours."

"Well, it was found at a crime scene. What can you tell me about the tag?"

"A yellow tag means it was issued in June. The boxed number 4 means there were 4 items cleaned for order number #631," the woman explained.

"Can you tell me who those items belonged to for that order number?"

"Yes, it is recorded in our June journal. It has already been billed out."

"I'll need the name and address of the person who brought in the clothing," said Cavallaro.

Hesitating briefly, the woman asked, "Are you going to tell anyone where you acquired this information from?"

"No, there isn't any reason to involve your business."

"That is good to know," she said, sounding relieved. I

will get it for you right away," she said.

"Thank you," said Cavallaro, grinning as he looked back at Parisi and whispered, "I told you. Really easy, isn't it?"

Parisi nodded his head in agreement. "I'm amazed," he said quietly.

Several moments later, the woman returned with a journal and placed it on the counter. She opened the book and flipped through several pages and said, "Here it is," pointing to the entry.

"Who does the tag belong to?" asked Cavallaro

"The items belong to customer #379. I have that information in another book. It is under the counter." Bending down, she brought up a smaller journal and flipped through several pages until she located #379. "Here it is," she said. "The customer's name is Moira Gray, 892 Crain Street, Evanston."

"Are you sure about that? Our suspect is a male."

"Yes, she is a regular customer."

"Is she married?"

"I do not think so. Maybe your suspect could be either a friend, or a boyfriend?"

"Yeah, maybe," he said.

"You are not going tell Ms. Gray where you heard this information from, are you?"

"No, but thanks for your help," he said. "I just need to

jot her name and address in my note pad and we'll be on our way. We won't bother you again unless we need something else."

"We are always happy to help the police," said the young woman.

"Thanks again," said Cavallaro. "Oh, can I have your name for our records?"

"Sure," she said. "I am Julie Wong, the owner's daughter."

"Thanks again Ms. Wong," said Cavallaro, as they walked out the door.

Chapter 9

When they got into the car, Parisi said, "I can't believe how easy it was to find out who the laundry tag was issued to. We should call Ricci right away and tell him we got a name and address for the tag."

"Yeah, he should be pleased," said Cavallaro.

I lost a certain amount of respect, trust, and credibility, in Don Ricci's eyes, when I screwed up in Saugatuck, thought Cavallaro. *Getting this information should help me to regain at least some of it back.*

The ringing telephone awakened Minello from his mid-morning nap. Still half asleep, he slowly answered the call. "Yeah, hello," said Minello.

"Paulie, tell Dominic we got a lead on the hit man," said Parisi.

"What'd you get?" questioned Minello.

"A name and address."

"That's good news. Dominic is not here, but I'll tell

him when he returns," said Minello.

"Who does the tag belong to?"

"The tag was issued to a local woman named Moira Gray. The clerk we talked to knows her, but didn't think she was married. She lives in Evanston not far from the cleaners. We got her address. She could be related to the hit man or be his girlfriend. Tony and I think we should stake out her house and see if a guy shows up."

"That sounds reasonable," said Minello.

"If we see a man at her house, what do you want us to do?"

"Are you certain about this information?"

"Yeah, we saw the records for ourselves. We posed as cops, and the clerk cooperated with us. We saw the information, in Wong's journals. No doubt about it. It has to be right."

"Okay, watch the residence, but don't do anything else until I get a chance to talk to Dominic. Understand?"

"Yeah, I got it. What if a guy shows up and Tony can verify he is our hit man? What do you want me to do then?"

"Nothing, just watch him for now."

"That's it?"

"Yes, and try not to attract any unnecessary attention while you're doing it Jimmy."

"I was thinking of renting a van to use for surveillance

purposes. What do you think?"

"Do what is needed, but don't be too conspicuous."

"What if our guy doesn't show up in the next few days?"

"You might need to question the woman. Do whatever you need to do, but remember, we don't want her killed."

"I got you," said Parisi. "Hopefully, we'll see our guy outside the home and not have to mess with the woman."

"Whatever, just be careful. We can't afford to make any more mistakes."

* * *

Moira got home Friday at five. She didn't notice the white van parked down the street in front of the neighborhood bar.

Bartlett had been in the house all Friday morning. The couple had said their goodbyes that morning before she left for work. In the afternoon, Bartlett departed through the backyard and headed for the airport. He had alluded to a three-day business trip to Washington, D.C. to officially conclude his business with the CIA. However, he had lied to her about the real destination and purpose of the trip. Instead of Washington, D.C., he planned a trip to the west coast in order to be absolutely consistent with his retirement plan to eliminate all loose ends, and to avoid capture.

Harsh Consequences

* * *

Since Friday afternoon, Cavallaro and Parisi had been staking out Moira's home. They had seen the same woman come and go several times over the weekend, but they had not seen a man. They assumed the woman was Moira Gray. Cavallaro doubted she was involved with the hit man. She didn't have the appearance of a typical criminal's woman due to her plain look and discouraging attire. She was cute, but not flashy. Instead, Cavallaro wondered if she were a relative.

Minello instructed them to wait until Monday evening to approach Gray if a man had not shown up by then. Late Monday afternoon, Parisi picked the lock at the back door and entered the house. Cavallaro waited in the van until after he saw Parisi signal the okay by turning the porch light on and off.

Once inside the residence, the men began to search the living room, where they found some old family pictures displayed on the wall. They noted the home was decorated with inexpensive furniture, a few antiques, and some family heirlooms. The spare bedroom was neat and tidy and was being used mostly for miscellaneous storage and seasonal clothing. The kitchen was bright and clean and there was a pleasurable fragrance in the room.

In the master bedroom, they did not find a framed photograph of a man displayed on her dresser. They looked in the clothes closet and saw only women's clothing. However, there were several men's items at one end of the closet. On the bathroom counter, there were several men's toiletry items, including condoms, and cologne, intermingled between women's products next to the sink. They carefully rummaged through the dresser drawers and found no letters, diary, or personal papers linking her to a special someone.

Before Parisi entered the home, he had peered through the locked garage door window where he saw a vehicle parked inside the building. However, it was dark and he could not tell the make or model of the automobile.

They had anticipated Moira to be home around five, so they waited for her in the second bedroom. At about five-thirty the front door opened and they heard someone walk into the house. A few minutes later, they could hear a woman's voice talking on the telephone. They waited to act until after she had concluded the call.

Quietly, Parisi opened the door, crept down the hallway, and carefully peered into the kitchen. Standing in front of the sink, was a slender, modestly dressed brunette rinsing off vegetables. Slowly, Parisi approached the woman from behind and said, "I have a gun pointed at your head. Keep your mouth shut and turn around slowly."

Moira was surprised and startled, but she turned around and stared at the small, olive-skinned man holding a gun. The sight of the weapon frightened her and she began to shake.

"Please don't hurt me," she said, whimpering slightly.

"Are you Moira Gray?" Parisi asked, as Cavallaro

entered the room.

Cavallaro's large size, presence, and intimidating expression distracted and scared her. She was momentarily speechless.

"Pay attention lady, and answer my questions," said Parisi, in a disturbingly controlled voice.

She paused and said, "Yes, I will. What do you want from me?"

"We just want to ask you some questions," Parisi said.

"Okay ...," Moira said, nervously.

"We don't intend to hurt you, but we will if you don't tell us what you know."

In a trembling voice, she said, "What do you want to know? I'm not important to anybody. I'm just a clerk in an attorney's office."

"Where is the man who lives with you?"

"I don't have any man living with me," she said.

"Why are there men's clothing hanging in your closet?" questioned Parisi.

"They belong to my boyfriend but he's not here right now. Why do you want to know about him?"

"You don't ask the questions bitch, we do," said Cavallaro, interrupting her.

Moira turned and stared into the large, Italian man's dauntingly dark eyes and said nothing. Cavallaro, bothered by her boldness, slapped her violently across the face. The blow slammed her back against the counter.

"When will he be back?" Cavallaro asked, fiercely peering into her eyes.

"I don't know. He said he'd be gone for a few days. I never know with him."

"What do you mean you never know with him?" Cavallaro said, again slapping her across the face.

"What's this about?" asked Moira.

"Don't worry about it, just answer the questions. I don't want to hurt you but ..."

Moira remained silent.

"What's his name," Parisi asked.

"Jim," she said, as the tears began to roll down her cheeks. "Are you from The Agency?"

"What Agency? What's his last name? I'm not going to ask you again."

To their surprise, Moira remained silent.

"Where does he live?" asked Parisi.

"I don't know. He moves around a lot."

"Bitch, if you don't start answering our questions, I'm going to hurt you real bad," Cavallaro said, before he punched her in the stomach. After he did, Moira bent forward and began weeping in pain.

"I've told you all I know. Now get the hell out of my house."

"We're not going anywhere until you tell us everything you know about your boyfriend," said Cavallaro.

"I've told you all I know," she said, between sobs.

"I guess we'll have to do it another way then. You are going to tell me about Jim or I'm going to keep hitting you until you talk," Cavallaro said, grabbing her and shoving her down onto a kitchen chair.

"Get your hands off me. Help! Help!" she screamed.

Cavallaro grabbed her around the throat as Parisi began taping her to the chair. After she was adequately secured, Cavallaro put a piece of duct tape over her mouth. "That should do it," he said. "Are you happy now?"

Moira sat motionlessly, taped to the chair. She noticed the large, menacing looking Italian was missing most of his right index finger.

"When you decide to stop screaming and answer our questions, I'll take the tape off. It's your choice. We got lots of time," he said, as he hit her once again in the face.

Moira thought she felt her neck snapping when his fist collided with her chin. Blood began to slowly drip from her cheek. The blow she had received was as hard as she had ever been hit. She felt like she was about to pass out. Her body ached as she continued to sob.

Cavallaro hit her again on the other side of her mouth and blood began to slowly drip, this time, from her upper lip. She could feel her teeth tingling with pain after the punch.

"Take it easy Tony, we don't want to kill her," Parisi said, grabbing the man's arm.

"You better believe I've made plenty talk this way," he said proudly, as he savagely stared at her. "She's a tough one, but she's going to talk. They always do," he said, as he hit her again.

I never knew how much of a sadistic thug Cavallaro had become, thought Parisi. He's always been a menacing character, but I never thought he was stupid too. If he doesn't stop hitting her so much, she is going to be really messed up or worse. I wonder what Don Ricci would do to him for not following orders?

Moira raised her head and gave Cavallaro another cold stare before he body punched her again on the left side, just below her ribs. Feeling excruciating pain from the punch, Moira wondered if he had broken one of her ribs.

"Are you ready to talk or do you want some more?" Cavallaro said, ripping the tape from her mouth.

She gasped and sobbed as the duct tape removed some of her skin.

"You were cute, but now your jaw is swollen and you're bleeding. You look like a real mess," he said. "If I were you, I'd tell us what we want to know. Why protect him? He's not here to help you now. I will keep hitting you all night in order to get you to talk, if I have to," said Cavallaro.

"Please, don't hit me anymore," she pleaded.

"Let's see what you have inside the blouse," Cavallaro

said, as he ripped it open and pulled up her brassiere. He looked at her breasts and admired them. "You have really nice tits. Maybe I'll fuck you before I leave."

"No, please don't," she pleaded. His name is Jim Sanders and he lives in an apartment complex in the Loop. If I tell you his address, will you leave me alone?"

"Yeah, if you're telling us the truth, you'll never have to worry about seeing us again."

"He lives in Chicago at 645 S. Harrison Street, apartment 425."

"Are you sure about the address?"

"I wouldn't lie about it," she said.

"No. I guess not," Cavallaro said. "But, if we find out you're lying, we'll be back to see you," he said, as he slugged her once again in the stomach.

Moira slumped forward in the chair, as blood seeped out of her mouth. Immediately, she felt weak and incoherent. She felt as if she were going to pass out.

"Tony, you need to stop," Parisi said. "You remember what Paul said, don't you?"

"Yeah, okay. I think she's telling us the truth."

"After that beating, I'd be surprised if she wasn't," Parisi snickered.

Cavallaro whispered to Parisi, "I think we should kill her. She'll be able to identify us if we don't."

"She doesn't know anything about us."

"Yeah, I know, but why run the risk?"

"I think she just passed out," Parisi said, as he looked over and saw her slumped in the chair. "We'll need to tape her mouth shut again, so she won't be able to scream when she wakes up. We don't want the neighbors to hear anything."

"I've got the tape," said Cavallaro.

"Thankfully, she's still alive. Just tape her mouth shut and we'll get the hell out of here," said Parisi.

"Yeah, okay," said Cavallaro.

I doubt if she makes it. I hit her more than hard enough to kill her, he thought. I think the last several body punches to the stomach really injured her badly. I wouldn't be surprised if she suffocates on her own blood. That would be fine with me, you don't have to worry about the dead ever talking. I can hardly wait to see her boyfriend again. I'm going to enjoy killing him once Dominic gives me the go ahead.

Chapter 10

It was eight o'clock when Bartlett's flight from Los Angeles to O'Hare International Airport landed. Bartlett quickly found his bag and hurried to grab a cab back to Evanston. He was tired and relieved to be home. Most of the business in Los Angeles was concluded. There were only a few more loose ends that needed to be handled.

Upon arriving at Moira's house, Bartlett unlocked the back door and went inside.

I wonder why there isn't a light left on for me. Moira probably had forgotten to do it before going to bed. I need to be quiet, so I don't wake her, he thought.

An LED light from the radio barely illuminated the room. Bartlett put down his bag and was getting a drink of water when a wheezing sound from behind him caught his attention. He was unclear as to where or from whom the sound had originated. Bartlett turned and quickly scanned the room. He was surprised to see no one in the kitchen. Sensing something was wrong; he took several steps forward and stopped to ready himself for an attack. He looked again and noticed a large inanimate object down on the floor. Immediately, he turned on the light and was shocked to see Moira duct-taped to an overturned kitchen chair. He quickly examined her noticing her face was bruised and beaten. There was dried blood on her jaw and a piece of duct tape covering her mouth. Her body was partially exposed from the waist up. He noticed some bruising on her stomach and side. It appeared she had been beaten and probably molested too.

Carefully, he removed the tape covering her mouth. Blood had already coagulated inside her throat and she looked barely alive. "Oh my God! Moira! Moira!" he screamed, as he jiggled her to try to wake her up. Slowly, Moira opened her eyes. She displayed only a feeble smile upon seeing his face. He checked her pulse and it was dangerously weak. Bartlett had seen the signs of impending death before, and he was scared. The mere thought of losing her made him tremble.

Moira looks like she's dying. I'm astounded how she could have ever survived the obvious traumatic attack. I need to do something to help her very quickly, he surmised.

Thoughts of what steps to take next overwhelmed him. Bending down, Bartlett gently removed the tape that secured her to the chair. Cautiously, he lifted her into his arms; carrying her to the bed, he carefully laid her down. Rage began to build inside him as he scanned the seriousness of her wounds. "You're safe now, I'm here," he said. "Who did this to you?"

She spoke faintly, but not loud enough for him to hear

her response. He leaned over and placed his ear next to her mouth. Moira was extremely weak, but she said, "Two men from The Agency. One guy was missing a finger. He kept hitting me. The other guy called him Tony."

I'm going to fucking kill those bastards is all he could think. Putting his arms around her, he held her for several seconds. "It's going to be alright. I'll take care of you," he said, wondering all along if it was too late.

"I love you," she said softly, as she lay peacefully in his arms.

"I love you too," he responded, as tears started to trickle down his cheeks.

"They wanted your name and address," she said, almost whispering. "I didn't tell them anything."

Suddenly, she began to wheeze more violently trying harder to breathe. He noted her skin color was beginning to change, and her heart rate was dropping dangerously. Jumping up, Bartlett quickly turned her on her side and began to clear the dried blood clots from her mouth. He wondered if her bronchial tubes were clogged too. Immediately, he responded by starting CPR, to help her breathe and to keep her heart functioning. Gradually, her breathing began to slow and he could barely detect a heart rate. Bartlett realized CPR was not working and that soon she would be dead.

Hysterically, he continued CPR yelling several times at her, "Don't go." A few moments later, Moira was gone. He continued CPR for 5 more minutes before he realized his efforts were no longer necessary.

Bartlett gently gathered her into his arms and rocked her back and forth as he wept and softly whispered, "Please come back to me Moira, please." After what seemed like an eternity, he laid her back down, placed a pillow under her head, and covered her half-naked body with a blanket. Through his tears, he gazed at her, understanding the love of his life had died and was gone forever. Emotionally exhausted, he continued to weep.

She'd be alive if she hadn't tried to protect me. I should have been here to protect her. I'm not going to be able to live with myself, he thought.

Moira's death reminded him of New Orleans and the death of his Army buddy, Benny Gentry.

Benny and Moira had been loyal to me until the end and now they are both gone, he thought. Life doesn't seem to be fair. I should have been killed instead of them, but they sacrificed themselves for me.

Bartlett had many enemies, but he immediately knew who was responsible for Moira's death. He had already dealt with Gentry's killer in New Orleans and now he would deal with hers, in Detroit.

He lay down next to her on the bed and embraced her, closed his eyes, and thought about her death.

If I call the police they will probably detain me and accuse me of killing her. During their investigation, they will discover my fake identity and put me in jail. In order to protect myself, I have no choice but to dispose of her body and make it appear accidental.

Bartlett removed her clothing and put a favorite negligée on her. He tenderly kissed her lips and forehead, caressed her hair with his fingers, and paused briefly to admire her beauty once again. He wanted more time to be with her, but knew he had no more time. Bartlett needed to act as quickly as possible. "I love you Moira," he said, looking at her for the last time.

Bartlett rushed to pack the remains of his clothing and toiletry items, before leaving the room. He glanced one more time at Moira before slowly closing the bedroom door.

In the spare bedroom, he removed the cover to an electrical outlet and loosened the wires, allowing them to arc inside the box. He went to the garage and retrieved a small propane torch he had used to repair a leak in one of the water lines.

Moira had purchased several gallons of paint to refresh some of the rooms. He stacked the cans in the bedroom, near the outlet, and used the torch to ignite the wood and insulation from inside the box. Once the fire started to erupt, he replaced the outlet cover and watched as the flames slowly began to burn through the plaster and wooded wall.

Bartlett knew as the fire grew, it would quickly destroy the small wood-framed home. He waited in the alley behind the garage until the flames were visible through the roof.

"Goodbye my love," he whispered. He knew under the

circumstances, it could not have ended any other way. After going several blocks, Bartlett turned again and watched as the blaze continued to grow, until he heard sirens approaching in the distance. He knew it would have only taken several minutes for Moira's body to be burnt beyond recognition. He hoped the authorities would conclude the fire resulted from a faulty electrical outlet.

With luggage in hand, he walked to a nearby motel and checked in. He placed his bags in the room and decided to wait a while to think and to try to regain his composure. Two hours later, Bartlett departed on foot for Pauline Hadley's home. He wanted to inform her about the fire and Moira's death.

* * *

Cavallaro and Parisi had arrived in downtown Chicago and were looking for 645 S. Harrison Street. When they came upon the address, it only took them a few seconds to determine the Italian restaurant, at that location, was not an apartment complex, as Moira had originally told them.

"That bitch lied to us!" said Parisi. "I can't believe it. Aren't you glad now that you didn't kill her?" he asked Cavallaro.

"Yeah. But, I can't imagine she's still alive," Cavallaro said. "Remember, I covered up her mouth with tape. I wouldn't be surprised if she suffocated on her own blood."

"If she's dead, Ricci will really be upset. Remember

what Paulie told us?"

"Yeah, I know," Cavallaro said.

"Maybe she's still alive. Let's go back and question her again," said Parisi.

* * *

Thirty minutes later, Cavallaro stopped the van about two blocks from Moira's residence. He could see a police barricade and fire trucks parked in front of her home. Cavallaro and Parisi got out of the van, walked to the barricade, and mingled with the crowd that had gathered, watching as the firemen extinguished the last of the flames.

To their amazement, it looked as if the home had been totally destroyed in the blaze. They wondered if Moira had been saved or if she was killed in the fire.

"What the hell?" Cavallaro said. "How could this have happened?"

"I don't know, but let's get the hell out of here. All these cops are making me nervous," said Parisi anxiously.

"Yeah, we better not hang around very long," said Cavallaro.

As they were leaving, Parisi questioned a nearby spectator, "Do you know if there were any survivors?"

"I wouldn't know," said the elderly gentleman, who apparently lived in the neighborhood. "But, if there had been someone inside, by the time the firemen arrived, it was probably too late. I've seen these older structures catch fire before and they seem to go down rather quickly," explained the man.

* * *

It was eleven o'clock at night when Pauline Hadley awoke to the musical chime of her front doorbell. She quickly got up, put on a robe, and cautiously approached the door. She turned on the porch light and nervously peered through the door's side panel window. To her surprise, there was a casually-dressed, handsome, middle-aged man, outside on the front porch.

Leaving the safety chain attached, she cracked the door and nervously asked, "What can I do for you sir?"

"Are you Pauline Hadley," Bartlett asked.

"Yes, who are you?

"I'm Jim Bartlett, Moira's fiancé," Bartlett replied.

"Do you know what time it is?" Pauline said acting mildly disturbed.

"Yes I do, but I have something very important to tell you. I'm sorry to have to tell you this, but there's been a terrible accident. Moira is gone. I don't know what to do. May I come in?"

"Yes, come in," she said, shocked by what she had just heard. "Tell me what happened."

"Moira's gone," he said again, with tears dripping from his eyes.

Pauline hesitated and then gasped when she realized what he meant by the word gone! "Oh my God! No!" she screamed. "What are you talking about? I spoke to Moira tonight after she got home from work, and she was fine."

"I don't know. When I got home from my business trip, about two hours ago, the house was totally engulfed in flames. It was a horrible fire and nothing was left. I assumed Moira was inside when the fire broke out. I asked several spectators, who were watching the fire, if they had seen any survivors. They said they had not. Nevertheless, I looked around aimlessly for her for thirty minutes before I took off. I've been walking around ever since not knowing what to do."

"Are you sure she was in the house?" asked Pauline.

"I talked with one of her neighbors who told me she had seen Moira inside the house several hours before the fire. As far as I know, she didn't have any plans this evening. That's why I'm sure she was at home."

"Did you talk to the police?"

"Not yet. I was afraid they would think I had something to do with starting the fire.

"Why would they think you had something to do with the fire?" Pauline asked, sounding puzzled.

"The authorities always accuse the spouse or the boyfriend in these types of circumstances."

"Well, you don't have to worry about it. You guys were not having problems. You were in love and soon to be married."

"Yeah, I guess you're right," he said. "But, I grew up never trusting the police. Nevertheless, she's gone," Bartlett said, as he started to tear up again. "What am I going to do without her?" he said, placing his face in his hands and sobbing.

Pauline reached over and patted him on the back. "I'm so sorry for your loss," she said, as she began to cry too. "What can I do to help?"

"I don't know," he said. "I can't believe this is happening. It doesn't seem real."

"I understand. Come out to the kitchen," she said. "I'll make us some coffee and we can talk there."

"Thanks. I'm not going to be able to sleep anyway," said Bartlett.

Pauline turned on the coffee maker and waited for it to percolate before she poured two cups of coffee. Handing one to Bartlett, she said. "I'm totally shocked. I can't believe Moira is dead."

"I can't either," Bartlett said, as he sighed. Did you say you talked to her tonight?"

"Yes."

"What did you talk about?" he asked.

"It was kind of strange. She asked me if I had told anyone your last name or where you lived."

"What did you tell her?" inquired Bartlett.

"I told her I hadn't. We chatted briefly about getting together for lunch later this week and that was about it. She told me what she was making for dinner and then said she had to go. Strange, now that I think about it, she acted as though she was uptight about talking about you."

"I wonder why she asked you about me?" questioned Bartlett.

"I have no idea. Incidentally, where are you staying tonight?" inquired Pauline.

"Probably in a motel, the house is gone," he said.

"You are welcome to stay here. My couch is pretty comfortable. In the morning, I'll get up and make us breakfast and we can go see the authorities together. I'll vouch for you. Everything will be fine. You'll see."

"I don't want to be any trouble for you. I can stay in a motel."

"No, stay here," she said. "I'll bring you a pillow and blanket."

"I guess it'll be alright," he said. "Thanks, I just don't want to be a bother to you."

"If you need anything else or want to talk, I'll be in the next room."

"Okay, thanks," he said, again. "Do you want more coffee?"

"Sure, I'll get it," she said.

"No, sit still," he said. "I'll pour you another cup." Bartlett got up, walked behind Pauline towards the coffee maker, turned, and placed his hands firmly on her head.

"What are you doing?" she screamed.

Without responding, he quickly broke her neck with one powerful snap. It only took a few seconds and Pauline collapsed in the chair. Bartlett picked her up and dragged her to the basement door. Opening the door, he turned on the light, and pushed her down the stairs. She went head over heels and landed several feet past the bottom of the stairway. He quickly wiped his prints off the door handle, grabbed his coffee cup, and departed out the back door.

Bartlett knew there was no other option with Pauline. She had known too much about his life. As far as he was concerned, his survival was more important than hers.

Unfortunately, another innocent person had to be sacrificed to atone for my past sins. I'm back in another war zone, and this time my mission is to avenge those responsible for Moira's death, thought Bartlett.

Chapter 11

Cavallaro and Parisi were surprised and shocked to see that Moira's home was totally destroyed. They assumed she was probably dead. Regardless, they knew they'd have to return to Detroit the following day and report the bad news to Minello and Ricci.

Around midnight, the men were having pie and coffee at a roadside diner contemplating whether they should phone Minello concerning the current situation. Due to the circumstances, they decided it would be best to make the call. Still, they were unprepared and too nervous to tell him about Moira's demise, early in the conversation.

"What did you find out?" Minello asked.

"We interviewed Gray several hours ago," said Parisi. "We discovered she is either a very good liar or had no idea about her boyfriend's criminal activities."

"What did she say?" Minello asked, somewhat puzzled by their answer.

"When we interrogated her, she asked if we were from

The Agency."

"What was that about?" asked Minello.

"We're not sure, but I've heard the CIA referred to as the Agency before," said Parisi. "When I first started talking to her, I got the feeling she didn't know very much about his life. Maybe he works for the CIA too."

"I doubt it, but I guess you never know," said Minello.

"After about fifteen minutes of persuading, she finally told us her boyfriend's name was Jim Sanders and that he lived in the Italian section of Chicago," said Parisi. "When we went to the address she had given us, it turned out to be an Italian restaurant instead of an apartment complex. I can't be certain that she lied to us or that she just didn't know for sure herself. Earlier, she commented that his schedule was not always predictable, which also made no sense."

"When you found out she had sent you to the wrong address, what did you do to her?"

Parisi paused and reluctantly said, "There was a problem. We'll be coming home tomorrow and you'll get all the details."

"What problem?" exclaimed Minello.

Hesitating briefly, Parisi finally spoke, "Once we discovered she had given us the wrong address, we returned to Evanston to talk to her again."

"Wait a minute, I'm confused," said Minello. "Wasn't she with you when you went to Sanders assumed address?"

"No. We left her at home duct-taped to a kitchen chair. Tony taped her mouth shut, so she wouldn't be able to scream."

"Really," said Minello.

"When we got back to Evanston, we discovered there had been a fire at her house. There were cops everywhere asking questions. We got nervous and decided to leave."

"How bad was the fire?"

"It was pretty bad," said Parisi.

"How bad was it?"

"The house was totally destroyed," said Parisi.

"What the fuck! Did you two start the fire?" screamed Minello.

"No. We didn't do it. We only did what I told you. Gray was alive in the kitchen when we left the house. I swear Paul! However, we haven't been able to verify if she died in the blaze or not. That's all we know," Parisi said.

"I see. That's fucking terrific," said Minello. "Dominic is not going to be happy. When you get back, I'm sure he'll want to talk to you right away. You better have a real good explanation."

"We will Paul. I'll let you know when we're back in town."

Minello laid down the receiver, thought about their conversation, and immediately called Ricci with the bad news.

"I want to see those two idiots as soon as they get back. Do you understand me Paul?" yelled Ricci.

"Yeah, I've already told them Dominic. "Do you want me to do anything else?"

"Yes, before I get in the office tomorrow morning, I want you to call your counterpart in Chicago. Ask him what he knows specifically, about our hit man."

"Anything else Dominic?"

"Don't get too specific about our situation; they don't need to know all our business."

"I'll take care of it. See you tomorrow."

* * *

It was early morning when Bartlett finally got back to the motel. Unbeknownst to him, Tony Cavallaro and Jimmy Parisi were across the street at an adjacent motel resting somewhat uncomfortably. Bartlett was distraught and exhausted, but he needed to think. His head was spinning, as he thought about the events surrounding Moira's death.

He knew Ricci's people were looking for him, and regrettably, Moira had somehow gotten in their way. It was not a twist of fate her assailant's name was Tony. Tony was the name of one of Ricci's soldiers. He remembered his first encounter with this man in Saugatuck about two months earlier.

The first time I saw him, he was in a white work van, parked at Haley's Marina. He was trying to look inconspicuous. Later, I learned he was there as part of an intricate plan to eliminate me, once I had killed State Senator Louis Stroh and his girlfriend, for the Ricci family. No doubt, Ricci's game plan was designed to cover up their involvement in the crime.

Tony told me it was his job to spy on Stroh and to kill me too. However, he had a major problem; he didn't know what I looked like. He was there watching Stroh and hoping to get a glimpse of me too.

The second time I saw him, he was near the Senator's residence and I questioned Wallace about his presence. I remember Wallace tried to explain away the situation by telling me a lie. He claimed Tony was a detective they had hired for a surveillance job just to monitor Stroh.

Initially, their contract with me contained an unusual twist, because I had been hired to setup a hit, but was told it may or may not be necessary. At the time, the arrangement sounded peculiar and simplistic. Later, when I questioned Wallace, he assured me if I was given the go ahead, the detective wouldn't be getting in my way. After being told to proceed, even though the detective was still there, I became suspicious and concerned. I wondered whether or not Tony's assignment involved more than just Stroh.

I remember becoming so troubled about the real purpose of his business, and continued presence, that I decided it was necessary to detain him and conduct my own interrogation. I ended up cutting off his finger and threatening to sever his hand before he finally began to cooperate and talk to me. It was interesting to find out Tony was more dedicated to the Riccis' than I had previously imagined. Tony told me he was related to Dominic Ricci, the boss of the Ricci family.

He confirmed my suspicions that I was being double-crossed when he told me that Ricci had ordered him to kill me once the contract was completed. I was surprised to learn that Ricci had underestimated my abilities and misjudged how difficult it was going to be to kill me. Also, I had imagined Tony would be a fairly tough character, but surprisingly he wasn't.

I considered killing him after the interrogation, but I decided it might be more advantageous to let him live. Ricci would accuse him of disclosing the plot and have him killed. In retrospect, I regret not following my instincts to slit the guy's throat. Moira might still be alive today if I had done it. If given a second chance, I'd never make that mistake again, thought Bartlett.

Bartlett knew Tony had beaten up Moira to get her to talk, but he wondered why she had been molested.

The guy must be some kind of sex maniac or an animal. I'm going to make that fat-assed Italian wish he had never touched her, Bartlett thought. Once I get ahold of him, I'm going to torture him and maybe castrate him, before I finish him off. He'll be begging me to kill him before I'm done.

Bartlett removed his clothing and got into bed.

Life can change at a moment's notice and not for the

best, he thought. Several hours ago, I was retired, happy, and intent on starting a new life with Moira. Now, everything has suddenly changed. I need to avenge her death and quickly.

Bartlett believed Ricci was probably after him because of the tape recording he had sent to the Prosecutor's office and for his failure to complete the contract.

Ricci should have known better than to try to double-cross a professional killer and brutalize, molest, and kill his girlfriend. He's made a big mistake and he's going to pay for it right along with his cousin Tony.

Not surprisingly, Bartlett could not sleep due to the events of the evening and the coffee. He lay in bed, imagining how much he was going to miss her. Tears began to form in his eyes again and he started to weep, as he imagined how frightening the last few hours of life must have been for her.

What am I going to do? My plans and dreams of retirement with her are over.

Bartlett tossed and turned for more than an hour before he was able to fall asleep. He awoke around nine o'clock and checked out of the motel, rode a city bus downtown, and got off at a side street café where he ate breakfast. As he sipped his coffee, he thought about Moira again and his situation.

I don't believe Ricci's men understood the importance of Moira to me. She paid the ultimate price protecting me.

Bartlett was grateful for her sacrifice, but saddened that

she had to pay for the sins of his vocation. As he continued to reflect on the situation, he knew his immediate threat might be coming from the authorities and not the mobsters. The police might be looking for Pauline Hadley's killer and maybe Moira Gray's too.

He assumed his former superior, Army 2nd Lieutenant David Coles, now a homicide detective assigned to a south-side Chicago precinct, probably would not be involved in either case. Bartlett recalled being caught by Coles and released the last time he had visited the City. He also remembered Cole's warning about never returning to Chicago again.

Evanston had its own police force with an investigatory staff. Bartlett had been thoughtful, cautious, and professional in making both incidents appear to be accidental. He was hopeful there were not any witnesses to either crime and that both cases would be quickly closed.

Chapter 12

Early that morning, Minello phoned Anthony Pataldo, the underboss of the Chicago Outfit. "My friend, how are things in the Windy City? This is Paul Minello."

"Yeah, I know. Things are good. What can I do for you Minello?"

"Do you remember when you gave me a list of your freelancers maybe six months ago?"

"Yeah, vaguely. Why?"

"We used the Chicago guy from JBS Personnel Services on a job. Do you know his name or where he lives?"

"Why do you want to know? Did you have trouble with him?" asked Pataldo.

"Yeah, there was a small problem. My boss wants to talk to him again," said Minello.

"You have his number, right?"

"Yeah, but he's never called us back," said Minello.

"Really? Normally he's prompt. The guy has done lots of work for us over the years."

"Great, do you know his name?"

"He goes by the name of John Moore but it's an alias. I suppose you know that he insists on absolute anonymity, but he is one of the best. Even we don't know his real name."

"Yeah, that's why we contacted him. We wanted the best," said Minello.

"Generally he's very efficient and timely. Most of our friends would highly recommend him."

"Are you telling me you don't know the guy's real name but you trust and freely recommend him anyway?" questioned Minello.

"Yeah, essentially that's right. Originally, some of the older guys knew his real name, but over the years it never got passed on. He never caused any problems, so nobody cared. The only guy who probably knew his real name is in a Cicero nursing home with Alzheimer's. I doubt if he could help you. What's this all about anyway?"

"My boss just wanted some more information about him."

"I'll give you what I know. I've heard he isn't Italian. They say he's Polish or Slavic. He was a highly decorated Vietnam veteran. I've been told he was a sharp kid from the south side who started in the business after the war. He is very ambitious and competent too."

"That's interesting," said Minello. "Okay, anything else?"

"He never works in Chicago anymore but we still know about his reputation. I've heard he sometimes partnered with a freelancer from Los Angeles. Do you want the guy's name and telephone number? Maybe he can help you."

"Yeah, sure. Go ahead and I'll jot it down," said Minello.

Pataldo gave him the information and said, "Glad to help. Incidentally, both of those guys have done plenty of jobs and they are very professional. I shouldn't have to warn you but don't ever consider crossing either one of them. They are known as being two of the best contract killers in the business. They are nobody to mess with, if you know what I mean."

"Yeah, I do. Thanks for the information. I'll talk to you later."

"Yeah, good luck," said Pataldo, as he hung up the phone.

I wonder what all the questions were about. We've heard about Ricci's trouble with the cops. He's supposedly up for attempted murder and kidnapping charges.

* * *

Mid-morning, Cavallaro and Parisi stop at a local newspaper stand and purchase a copy of the Evanston edition of the Chicago Tribune. They were particularly interested in the article on page eight. The headline read, "Woman Dies In Fire." According to the story, Moira Gray, a 50-year-old Crane Street resident was killed in a late night blaze that totally destroyed her house. The Evanston Fire Department's preliminary report suggested an electrical problem was responsible for the fire. Her remains have been taken to a local funeral home and arrangements are pending.

Parisi read the article and placed the newspaper inside his duffle bag to show Ricci. The article was proof the woman had died as a result of the blaze.

On the same page but near the bottom was another article about a death in Evanston. According to the story, a woman had fallen down her basement steps and died from a broken neck. Parisi had scanned over the article but had no reason to believe the two deaths were connected.

* * *

Mid-afternoon, the two mobsters arrived back at the Military Surplus business. They went inside and met Ricci at his office door. Cavallaro could immediately tell Ricci was very upset.

"Sit down over there," he pointed to the men. "I want an explanation!"

"Okay Dominic," Cavallaro said, nervously.

"I can't believe I trusted you two idiots to handle this task. I've heard things got fucked up again," he said. "I told you not to kill the woman, but she's dead. What the hell happened?"

"We didn't kill her, she died in a fire. We have a newspaper article here with the story to prove it. The fire department said it was an accidental fire caused by an electrical problem. Why are you blaming us?" Cavallaro asked.

"Because this fire probably wasn't an accident," Ricci said. "The son-of-a-bitch is going to come after us with a vengeance because his girlfriend is dead. He'll hold us personally responsible for her death," he said, as he reached into his desk drawer and pulled out a .38-caliber snub nose revolver. "I think I'll do him a favor and kill you myself," he said, pointing the gun at Cavallaro.

"Dominic, you might want to wait," said Minello. "Tony claims it wasn't their fault. Maybe we should hear his side first."

"We've already heard the explanation. The facts are the woman is dead, and they had some part to play in it," Ricci said, pausing briefly to think. "Okay, if it wasn't your fault then whose fucking fault was it Tony?"

"I don't know Dominic, but it wasn't our fault. We didn't kill her. I smacked her around a little to get her to talk but not enough to kill her. She was really scared. We assumed she was telling us the truth about her boyfriend. When we left her house, she was still alive and securely duct-taped to a kitchen chair. The woman was a lot more clever and courageous than we could have imagined. The address she gave us was phony and probably his name too. When we went back to confront her about it, we discovered her house was engulfed in flames."

"Did you start the fire?" Ricci asked.

"Hell no we didn't. And, we don't know who did. When we left she was still alive in the kitchen," Cavallaro insisted.

"Maybe the hit man came home after you left. He found her tied up and asked her what happened. Perhaps after he heard her explanation, he freaked out and decided to kill her. Am I to believe, he started the fire before he left too?" said Ricci.

"I don't know Dominic," said Cavallaro.

"Maybe he did it to protect himself," said Ricci.

"Yeah, maybe because she had become a liability," said Cavallaro, theorizing.

"It's possible," said Ricci.

"I don't know Dominic," said Cavallaro. "I know it sounds like we killed her but we didn't do it."

"No, why would we? She gave us the information we asked her for," interjected Parisi.

"Why didn't one of you stay with her until you could verify she was telling you the truth?"

"She was tied up. We didn't think it would be a big problem to leave her alone there. Besides, if we'd been able to find the hit man, I figured it would be better to have two of us on him, instead of one. I'm sorry things got messed up," said Cavallaro.

"Well, thanks to the two of you, we are all going to be screwed," said Ricci. "Get the hell out of here before I change my mind about shooting you."

"I'm really sorry Dominic," said Cavallaro, as he and Parisi quickly walked out of the room.

Several moments later, Ricci turned to Minello and asked, "Do you believe their story, Paul?"

"I think so Dominic. Parisi has always been a stand-up guy. But, you know Tony better than I do. He's your cousin. What do you think?"

"I don't know if he's lying or not. For his mother's sake, I hope not," said Ricci.

"What's our next move Dominic?"

"I want to think about it some more but I know John Moore, or whoever the hell he is, will be coming for us now," said Ricci. "Still, there is something about their story that just doesn't make any sense. If she were alive when he arrived, wouldn't he have taken her with him, instead of burning her up in the home? What if the woman was dead before Moore came home and found her? If she were dead, he'd only start the fire to destroy the evidence to protect himself. That makes more sense, doesn't it?"

"Yeah, it does," said Minello. "Want me to kill them?"

"No, just keep your ears open. We need to know if we can trust them."

After their meeting with Parisi and Cavallaro, Minello told Ricci that Pataldo had provided them with very little information to help them find Moore. However, he had mentioned that a Bill Morgan, from Los Angeles had worked with him in the past. Dominic wasn't too happy about the news. He instructed Minello to contact Morgan to see if he could help. When Minello called Morgan's telephone number, he was disappointed that no one answered his call. He left a short message with his name and number on the answering machine.

Minello's main problem was that neither he, nor Pataldo, knew John Moore's real name. This will obviously make it more difficult to track him down.

It's hard to believe these mob guys are entrusting people to do this work, yet nobody knows their real names. It was different in the old days. Everybody knew everyone, but these days, with the concern for anonymity, reputation, performance, and efficiency, those were the only things that really mattered anymore. Minello thought, if he were running the mob, he would insist, to those he was interested in hiring, that they divulge all information, or risk not getting the job.

He reported the news about Morgan to Ricci, who was already irritated and frustrated. Upon hearing the news, Ricci pivoted and said to Minello, "Send somebody to Chicago and see if they can locate Franklin D. Russo and find out what he knows. Start at the Kenilworth building. Somebody there has to know something. JBS would have kept records. We need to find them. But, don't send Cavallaro or Parisi. This time, I want to make sure our leads remain alive, in case we need something else from them. That shouldn't be too hard ... should it?" said Ricci, sarcastically.

Minello answered, "No, it shouldn't be too hard Dominic. I'll see to it personally. We can't afford any more mistakes."

"These people lead double lives," shouted Ricci. "Somebody has to know them."

"I agree Dominic. I'll make sure we find out something."

"Good, maybe you'll get lucky this time. Call Pataldo back and ask him if he has another phone number for John Moore or the other guy, Bill Morgan."

"I've already asked him and he doesn't know about either one of them having another phone," said Minello.

Chapter 13

Tuesday morning, Bartlett decided to go back to St. Croix and plan his revenge there, rather than in Chicago.

He called the airlines and quickly arranged for a flight back to Christiansted. Bartlett wanted to be out of Chicago as soon as possible, in case the police or the mobsters were hot on his trail. His outbound flight was scheduled to depart the following morning. Bartlett hailed a cab to the airport, and upon arriving, checked into the Belton International Hotel.

He was heartbroken that Moira was gone. It was similar to when he had seen Michael Killian, a close Army buddy, die in one of those nameless battles in the Vietnam War. Early on he learned that if you wanted to survive on the battlefield, there was not any time to grieve. In spite of his emotions, Bartlett learned it was necessary to try to desensitize and compartmentalize himself from the tragedies of war, in order to keep his sanity. Still, he was haunted by some of those incidents too brutal and horrible to forget.

Moira had not died in a real war. She had been thrust into a different kind of conflict through her association with him. Bartlett was having trouble handling her death, because of his absence and failure to keep her safe. Besides grieving her loss, he thought his guilty conscience was keeping him from sleeping at night.

Prior to lunch, Bartlett had bought some over-the-counter sleeping pills. He hoped the sample packet would be enough to help him rest. After lunch, he returned to his hotel room, climbed into bed, and attempted to sleep. His thoughts continued to be about Moira and those responsible for her death.

After thinking about his options, Bartlett realized the Ricci Family was not going to be leaving Detroit, it was their home base. And, the absence of an immediate retaliation might lull them into becoming more complacent. He was convinced that, if he waited a month or so before retaliating on the assailants, it might be easier for him to get retribution for her death.

* * *

Wednesday evening, Bartlett unpacked his bag and took a warm, relaxing shower. He was surprised he had been able to nap during the flights from Miami to St. Croix. However, he was extremely troubled by how quickly Ricci's men had been able to locate him. And, he was still very distraught and saddened by her death.

The only consoling thing Bartlett could recall about Moira's passing was the aura of calmness when she died. He was thankful she seemed to feel safe and comforted once he returned. Nonetheless, he still felt guilty and responsible because he had not been there to protect her.

I should have never left her alone and unprotected, he thought, once again.

Thursday morning, Bartlett awoke sluggish and unrested. He had tossed and turned all night and had slept only a few hours. On his way to work, Bartlett stopped by the pharmacy to buy some more sleeping pills. With the help of the pharmacist, he selected a different, and supposedly more effective, brand. The pharmacist told him to consider seeing a doctor if this brand did not work any better for him. Bartlett had not been to a doctor in years but he considered the recommendation sensible. He was able to sleep sporadically following Moira's death but it was not enough. Bartlett rarely ever had trouble sleeping. He wondered if the sleeping issues were a sign of a mild case of depression.

I'll need to have a very resourceful plan to get to Ricci now that the element of surprise is gone. But, I won't be able to develop anything actionable until my sleeping problems are resolved.

Bartlett knew Ricci was going to be well prepared to protect himself. He wondered what Ricci's plans might entail and how difficult it was going to be to get to him.

Maybe I can rely on Cavallaro's weaknesses again to help me.

Thursday night he tried the newer sleeping pills, but there was no improvement. After several days of similar results, Bartlett decided to consult a doctor at the clinic.

The St. Croix outpatient clinic was adjacent to the hospital. Bartlett walked into the clinic and, after talking with the on-call doctor, he agreed to a routine physical exam. The exam uncovered no physical problems but the doctor inquired if there had been any recent significant changes in his life. Bartlett told him there had been one major change and questioned whether it might be causing him trouble. The doctor seemed to be understanding and suggested, on a temporary basis, he might try a stronger dose of sleeping pills. Over several days, Bartlett could see some improvement.

Upon his return to the island, Bartlett told Rosa that he was suffering from flu-like symptoms and did not want her to be exposed to his germs. He decided it would be a good idea to temporally stay away from the Ursula Shop, and Rosa, in an effort to conceal the anxiety associated with Moira's death. She called several times to check on him, and he assured her his condition was improving. Naturally, he had no intention of telling her about Moira's death. Instead, he planned to tell her, if she ever inquired, the relationship had become too complicated and they decided to break-up. He was fairly certain Rosa might be happy to hear about their split. Her increased concern for his welfare made Bartlett think she wanted to be more involved in his life.

I am not ready for another relationship, he thought. It's way too soon. Although it's nice to know that someone else cares about me.

Monday morning, Bartlett strolled into the Ursula Shop. "Good morning," he said.

"It's nice to finally see you again," said Rosa, very sincerely. "It seems like it's been forever since you left for the States. Are you feeling better?"

"Yes, I feel better than I did. Have we received any packages from the Mainland?"

"Yes, UPS delivered four boxes yesterday. I put them on your desk," she said. "More merchandise?"

"Yes, and some personal stuff too. As soon as I get them priced, I'll give them to you to display. I think I bought some very nice things. They should sell easily."

"I'm sure," she said. "You have very good taste."

"Thanks," he said. "I'd like to work in the office today. There's a lot to do."

"I'll leave you alone all day," she said.

He always wants to be left alone to catch up when he returns from a trip, she thought. I take care of the business stuff; I wonder what kinds of things he has to do?

"You know me like a book, don't you Rosa," said Bartlett, grinning.

"I guess I do," she said.

If you'd ever give me a chance, I'd like to get to know you even better. He looks tired. I wonder if he is still sick.

At four o'clock Bartlett emerged from the office and

told Rosa he was tired and was going home to rest. She inquired again about his condition, and he told her he felt fine and would see her the following day.

Bartlett entered the shop the next morning, grabbed a cup of coffee, and gulped it down. "Good morning," he said.

"How are you feeling, Mr. Bartlett? I hope you're better," she said, sounding genuinely concerned.

"I'm better but not quite back to normal."

"Maybe you should go see a doctor. The clinic opens at eight. You might need a prescription."

"I already did see a doctor but maybe I should go back," he said. "I'll think about it at lunch."

* * *

Dr. Dennis Goggins, a semi-retired, internal medicine physician, originally from Boston, was the principal owner/operator of the out-patient clinic in Christiansted. Several days earlier, he had attended to Bartlett and his sleeping problems. Dr. Goggins suspected Bartlett was going through a life crisis of some kind and was experiencing signs of depression. The doctor had suggested a return visit if his sleeping failed to improve. Several days later, Goggins was not surprised when Bartlett returned.

Entering the examination room, Goggins politely

greeted Bartlett and asked him to sit, suggesting they talk for a while. "How did the prescription work for you?" he asked.

"The pills seemed to help but I still feel anxious and tired."

"Okay," Goggins said. "The other day you told me there had been a major change in your life. Can you tell me about the event?"

Hesitating for a moment, Bartlett said, "Well ... I was engaged to be married and my fiancée decided, at the last moment, that she didn't want to get married. Our relationship of course has suffered, but we've decided to remain friends and give it some time. Still, it has been very hard not to have her in my life," said Bartlett.

"Relationships are complicated. I had a relationship that didn't work out too well also. It's not fun, but it's better to find out now, rather than after you're married."

"Yeah, I suppose you're right."

"Mr. Bartlett, may I call you Jim?"

"Sure, if you want too."

"Jim, I think you're experiencing some symptoms that would indicate a mild case of depression. I'd like to prescribe Prozac, which is a more suitable drug to help manage your symptoms, instead of the sleeping pills. It's the most common drug used today for anxiety. I'd like you to take a 20 milligram capsule once a day for two months. There are side effects, but most people do fine, for a limited time, on this medication. I would like to see you again in two weeks to check on how you're doing. In the meantime, if you experience any of the serious side effects listed in the prescription material, please call me immediately."

"Thank you doctor," Bartlett said. "I'll call if I have problems."

An hour later, Bartlett decided to take the rest of the day off after his appointment with Goggins. He stopped at the pharmacy to pick up the new prescription and phoned Rosa to let her know he was done for the day. When he got home, he took the capsule and laid down for what he considered a well-deserved nap. When he awoke, he made himself some dinner and went immediately back to bed. The following morning he noticed no significant change in his sleep. However, he remembered the doctor had said the prescription would take at least a week to begin working.

A week later, the effects of the drug were beginning to become apparent. Bartlett was sleeping better but he still seemed to be experiencing some feelings of anxiety. When Bartlett began responding to imagined noises, in the house and outside on the porch, he felt worried, confused, and paranoid. He wondered if he should even be on the drug. Twice, he had awakened in the middle of the night, sweating profusely, after experiencing some really strange dreams.

The next day, Bartlett was out on the porch, taking an afternoon nap, when he unconsciously began to hear the sound of a grenade exploding. He envisioned himself reacting to the attack and immediately sought cover by some trees. A few moments later, he could see that one of his buddies, Private Michael Killian, was dead. He had been blown to bits by the explosion. Blood, and pieces of Michael's flesh, had flown in every direction. After the attack ended, Bartlett looked down and saw several pieces of Michael's body lying on the ground. He stared at a bloody, jagged arm and watched as the fingers continued to move. Reacting habitually in the battlefield, he got up and ran toward the elusive enemy, purposely firing his weapon at the fleeing Viet Cong. When he came upon the wounded enemy, responsible for throwing the grenade, Bartlett did not hesitate to put a bullet into the back of his head. The man's skull was partially blown apart when the bullet entered its intended target. When the dead man arose and ran back towards the jungle, it shocked and surprised Bartlett. He knew it was a wartime experience but parts of the event had somehow been grotesquely transformed and unrealistically altered.

Seconds later, Bartlett abruptly awoke and looked around the porch. He realized he was not back in the jungle and that he had been experiencing either another bad dream or a hallucination. At that moment, Bartlett decided to quit taking Prozac.

He phoned the doctor's office and immediately cancelled his next appointment. The nurse advised him to keep the appointment but he declined.

Within a week, Bartlett began to notice he was feeling and sleeping much better. He decided it was time to begin moving on without Moira in his life. She was gone and would never be back. Previously, he had decided to concentrate on avenging her death, finding another place to live, and resetting some of his retirement plans and priorities. Bartlett knew he would always have the loving memories of her to cherish, but he still had to live his life. Moving away from St. Croix and relocating elsewhere was not an appealing choice, but Bartlett understood changes needed to be made for his own protection.

Chapter 14

At six o'clock in the evening, Sarah Sloan locked her office door, turned off the reception area lighting and poured herself another cup of coffee. Every couple of weeks, Sloan stayed late to examine the stack of client folders that normally accumulated on top of her desk. She methodically reviewed each folder to make sure her services had been billed out before putting them back into the client filing cabinet.

When she noticed Moira Gray's folder in the stack, a somber look appeared on her face. She remembered reading the news story detailing the tragic death of her former client. Moira had been in therapy with Sloan, on an as-needed basis, over the past several years. Sloan was Moira's psychologist. She had been working with Moira on how to reestablish trust in new relationships after a divorce.

Sloan scanned the documents inside the folder and briefly stopped to reread the newspaper articles about the house fire and obituary notice included with her treatment notes.

She thought it odd that Moira's boyfriend had not been listed as a survivor. It had been over two months since Sloan had spoken to Moira, so she was not sure if the couple were still together or not. She had considered calling the funeral home to find out the boyfriend's name and address, to express her sympathy, but she decided against it. After all, she did have an ethical concern due to the client/therapist relationship. She did not know if the boyfriend knew Moira had been undergoing counseling or not. Sarah did not want to betray her deceased client's trust, either way.

On the same page, where the Gray story had appeared, was another news item concerning Pauline Hadley, who had apparently died from an accidental fall at her home. Sloan had known about Moira's friendship with Hadley but had completely forgotten her and their connection. The Evanston Police Department did not check either case too well, because they were short-staffed and had other more pressing crimes to solve. Both the Gray and Hadley cases were processed fairly quickly and closed.

* * *

Back in Detroit, Dominic Ricci sat at his desk thinking about the information they had compiled on John Moore. Thus far, he was displeased and extremely perplexed with the apparent lack of information. There was no information as to the whereabouts of Moore, the hit man who Wallace had hired for their job. No one in the Chicago Outfit seemed to have much information about him either. They also did not have any physical description, current address, phone number, or the real name of the man Ricci was seeking.

Twenty-five years before, John Moore had been sanctioned by several established mobsters from the Chicago area. Two years later, Moore had requested total anonymity as a condition of employment and the Chicago mob boss had approved, based on Moore's exemplary performance record. Apparently, the only people who did know anything about John Moore were Moira Gray, his newly deceased girlfriend, and an old-time Chicago mobster with Alzheimer's disease.

Minello sent two men to try to locate Franklin D. Russo, the man who Wallace had originally contacted in Chicago, to arrange a meeting with Moore. He was missing along with his girlfriend and they were both presumed to be dead.

The JBS Personnel Services office in the Kenilworth building was still vacant and the other tenants in the adjacent offices were of little help. Several of the tenants claimed they saw Russo sometimes in the mornings and that he had few visitors, with the exception of a few slutty-looking women who periodically appeared.

There were no public records for the business, except for some office rental receipts, phone book listings, and utility contracts that had long since been cancelled.

Minello learned Russo had paid all of JBS bills in cash.

The lawyer and private investigator, who Minello had sent to Chicago, returned in less than a week with nothing helpful to report. Apparently, the business had never filed an income tax return, and there were no business or personnel records available that they could find. The private investigator could not develop any meaningful leads either. They both commented it was as if JBS Consulting, Russo, and Moore, had never existed.

The attorney did learn that a John Bartkowski had, years earlier, changed his name to John Moore but the trail ended there. Moore had somehow vanished without leaving any remaining clues as to his whereabouts. They found out that John Bartkowski had been an Army veteran but was not receiving any Veteran's Administration benefits to date. Therefore, his current address was not available through the VA.

Upon reviewing Minello's progress report, Ricci was stunned.

How the hell could this be? John Moore isn't a ghost. There has to be more information about him somewhere, thought Ricci. I guess we will have to keep looking until we find something.

Several hours later, Ricci called Minello and told him to temporarily stop looking for Moore and start concentrating on Wallace. "After all, Wallace's knowledge could be more damaging to the family than the hit man," Ricci reminded Minello. "He betrayed me once before, and he might be trying to do it again with this latest threat."

"Yeah, I agree. We shouldn't trust him again."

"Are we following Wallace?" Ricci asked.

"Yes, we've been watching him since his release from the County jail, said Minello.

"Good," said Ricci. "Paul, I've been thinking about how we might be able to get our paperwork back from Wallace. What if we kidnap Samantha Parker, Wallace's attorney, and threaten to kill her if she doesn't cooperate with us? What do you think?"

"Are you sure that's a good idea? She is a lawyer and an officer of the court," said Minello.

"Well, what I'm sure of is that Wallace has told her things about himself that he hasn't told us. Maybe we could convince her to help us. You know, work with us behind the scenes."

"Yeah, it might work," commented Minello, reluctantly.

"Let's watch her for a while and get familiar with her schedule. She'd probably be pretty easy to snatch. Tony could take her to one of our abandoned buildings out in the warehouse district, stick his 9mm down her throat, and offer her a proposition. Either you agree to work for us or else we're going to blow your head off. All she'd have to do is find out what Wallace knows and what he is doing. For her help, we'd give her an envelope full of cash, and we'd let her live. We would remind her, nobody would ever have to know about our arrangement."

"What if she says yes but then goes to the cops?" questioned Minello.

"Tell her, if she ever decided to go to the cops, we'd know immediately and kidnap her son. We'd tell her if she didn't cooperate with us, she'd never see her son alive again. But, if she wanted to cooperate with us, nothing will happen to her or the kid. Nobody would be the wiser."

"It might work Dominic, but let's use someone other than Tony to handle this thing. Let one of my men take care of this. I want to make sure it's done right."

"That's fine with me if you want to handle it, but keep me posted on your activities. Understand?"

"Thank you Dominic. I understand, and I'll keep you informed," said Minello.

Chapter 15

Monday morning, Sammie Parker carefully pulled her shiny, new, Mercedes convertible out of the garage, promptly at seven-thirty. After a lazy weekend excursion to Petoskey, in Northern Michigan, Parker was relaxed, refreshed, and ready for work.

She had scheduled several court appearances to attend to after dropping off her ten-year-old son, Kevin, at St. Jude's Elementary School. The parochial school was located in the upscale neighborhood of Birmingham, Michigan, where Parker resided.

Ms. Parker was a tall, curvy, brunette beauty, originally from Grand Rapids, Michigan. She attended the University of Michigan Law School in Ann Arbor, and graduating with honors. While in Ann Arbor, she met and married George Parker, her former husband.

George Parker and Samantha Sullivan dated, eventually moving in together, two years prior to the announcement of their unplanned pregnancy. Upon learning the news, George immediately proposed marriage and Sammie accepted. The couple was together for almost eleven years before Sammie discovered George was having an affair with a young office associate.

The divorce turned out well for Sammie. After an ugly and drawn out legal battle, she settled with almost financial independence once the assets of George's commercial ventures were split. But, she was saddened by the way the divorce had adversely affected their son.

Kevin eventually began separating himself from his father as well, due to the traumatic divorce proceedings. Emotionally, Sammie was somewhat supportive of his response but realized her son still needed a relationship with his father. Her self-worth, and normally trusting nature, had been seriously shaken. Sammie felt rejected, and as a result, became vengeful, bitter, and withdrawn.

It had been more than a year since the divorce was final and Sammie had unexpectedly met an attractive, kind-hearted man, who was a professional football player. Kurt Slidell had come on the scene, completely unforeseen, and Sammie had been won over by his marvelous physique, character, intellect, and southern charm. She had always been used to the attention and affection of good-looking men, and Kurt seemed ideal. He was the perfect lover, friend, and companion and was divorced, childless, and five years younger. To Sammie's surprise, they fell in love immediately.

At a quarter till eight, Sammie pulled up at St. Jude's Elementary and gave Kevin the usual kiss and expectations before leaving for work.

Unbeknownst to her, there were two nefarious characters in a vehicle across the street who had been watching her every move since she had pulled out of the garage. Both men were Ricci family soldiers, working for Paul Minello, and they were assigned to follow her.

* * *

In St. Croix, Jim Bartlett got out of bed, and felt pretty good. *I'm feeling almost rested, he thought.* Even thought, he still felt awful about losing Moira, the persistent anxiety associated with her death was finally beginning to fade.

As he enjoyed his coffee, Bartlett reflected on several decisions he had already made concerning his future. He knew it would be wise to relocate somewhere else, hopefully in the Caribbean, sell the Ursula Shop and his home, and finalize his revenge plans.

Since the bulk of his funds were already in the Cayman Islands, he tentatively thought about touring Georgetown, in Grand Cayman, to evaluate the possibility of moving there. However, the Cayman Islands are a British territory and he wondered if moving there might be problematic. All of his documentation showed him as a United States citizen. In the future, he wondered if his frequent trips from the Cayman's to the United States might be more closely monitored and questioned than when he lived in the Virgin Islands.

His plans for revenge were finally coming together.

Bartlett was contemplating visiting Tony Cavallaro first, before finally meeting with Don Ricci, the person essentially responsible for Moira's death. In the past, Bartlett had successfully persuaded Cavallaro to rat on the boss, and he decided it might be worth a try again.

As for Ricci, Bartlett had thought about first trying to extort money from him, supposedly in exchange for his life. Although, he wondered if a Mafia Don would fall for such folly, from a renegade hit man. He doubted it but thought it might be a worthwhile strategy to pursue. After all, he could never have too much money in retirement. Regardless, Bartlett knew if the strategy either worked or failed, Ricci was still going to be dead.

Bartlett decided to do nothing more to Wallace since he had already implicated him in the Stroh matter with the taped recording. He thought it would be ample punishment for his involvement in the double-cross. Besides, he did not blame Wallace for Moira's death.

At ten o'clock Bartlett headed to a favorite seaside café in Christiansted for breakfast not far from his work. More recently, he had been trying to make a daily appearance at the Ursula Shop and had managed to catch up on most of his personal work. Rosa appeared happy to see him back in the shop and doing better. Bartlett knew she had been worried about his health, and now he was beginning to think more seriously about a relationship with her.

Just before noon Bartlett arrived at the shop. "Good morning," he said to Rosa, as he closed the back door.

"Good morning," she responded. "It's nice to be seeing

you on a regular basis Mr. Bartlett. I've really been concerned about you."

"Thank you," he said. "I'm glad that I'm feeling better too."

"I was beginning to wonder if your condition was more serious than you were letting on."

"No, fortunately it was only a really bad case of the flu."

"I was worried there was something more than that affecting you. You haven't been yourself lately," she said.

"To tell you the truth, you're partially right. I have been contemplating how best to share something with you concerning the shop," said Bartlett.

"Am I doing something wrong Mr. Bartlett?" Rosa asked nervously.

"No, on the contrary Rosa, this is not bad news. Things have changed in my relationship with Moira. We have decided there are too many complications in maintaining a long distance relationship. Neither one of us is willing to move, so the shop presents a major problem."

"Are you thinking about selling the shop and moving off the island?"

"Well, yes and no. I'd like to make you a ... well, let's say an unusual proposition, which I think you should strongly consider. I want you to be my partner in The Ursula Shop."

"How could I do that Mr. Bartlett? I don't have any

money," she said, with a puzzled look on her face.

"You don't, but I do. I'd like you to permanently run the shop by yourself. You're practically doing it anyway," he said. "I'd give you a substantial pay raise and I would allocate some of the shop's profit to you, so you could buy the shop. How does that sound to you?"

"It sounds like an incredible opportunity but why not just sell the shop to someone else? You'd be money ahead."

"I've thought about it, but I have grown to really like you and your dedication to the shop. According to my calculations, you could totally own the business in less than ten years."

"Mr. Bartlett, I'm flattered and shocked that you would be willing to help me like this. You have no idea how grateful I am to have you as both my boss and my friend."

"Thank you Rosa, but you deserve the praise," said Bartlett. "The arrangement I've worked out is outlined in detail on several spread sheets that I have prepared for you. I want you to study these documents," Bartlett said, handing Rosa a sealed manila envelope. "Review the enclosed information and let's talk again soon. As you will see, your share in the business will grow after each monthly payment is made to me. Your increased share of the profits every month will allow you to pay me off over time. You see, I don't really want to sell the business right now, and I don't need the money immediately either. It would please me greatly if you'd be willing to consider my offer."

"I'm totally stunned. I'll gladly review the information, but I'm sure I'll have some questions," she said.

"The next time we meet, I'll happily answer all of your questions and concerns."

"Okay," she said, "That sounds fair to me."

"While we're on the subject, I have only one request if you decide to enter into this partnership agreement with me. I want this arrangement to be kept strictly confidential. My accountant has advised me it would not be advantageous for me to divest my holdings in St. Croix right now. It's kind of involved and I really don't want to go into any more detail than that. So, please consider my request as you are thinking about my proposal."

"I certainly understand, and I truly appreciate the opportunity you are giving me. I won't tell anyone."

"Thank you Rosa. I'd like to have your decision as soon as possible," he said.

"Alright, I'll try to be ready sometime early next week."

"That sounds good to me," he said.

* * *

Back in Detroit, Paul Minello is eating a slice of pizza when the telephone rings. He answers the call. "How is the surveillance on Parker going?" he asks.

"We have been watching her for most of the day."

"What has she been doing?"

"She dropped her kid off at school this morning, headed downtown, and went inside the Courthouse. She was in there for several hours and then met a big guy for lunch. The way she was acting he was probably a boyfriend, or someone close."

"Find out who he is."

"How am I supposed to do that?"

"That's your problem. She'll probably see him again. Just figure it out. I want to know everything about her," barked Minello.

"Okay, we'll see if we can identify him. Anyway, after lunch she went back to her office and she's been there ever since. Have you seen her? She's a real looker."

"Yeah, I know, but keep you mind on the work."

"We will Paul," said the mobster, sensing a more than usual seriousness in his boss's attitude. "How long do you want us to watch her?"

"I want you to watch her until she turns off her lights and goes to bed, and keep watching her until I tell you to stop. I want a written report of where she goes, who she's with, and what she does every day. Got it?"

"Yeah, sure Paul, I just thought I'd ask. I didn't realize you wanted this much information about her. What's this about anyway?"

"Hey, just do your job! Don Ricci wants to know as

much as possible about her. That's all you need to know," Minello said intensely.

"No problem Paul. We'll do our job." *Don Ricci must really be pressuring him these days, thought the mobster. I wonder what is going on.*

Chapter 16

At three-thirty in the morning, Bartlett awoke in the midst of another disturbing dream about the night Moira had died. His t-shirt was drenched, and he could smell the stale odor of his perspiration. Lately, his recurring wartime nightmares were being replaced by her images.

In the dream, Bartlett recalled seeing her on the floor, duct-taped to a chair, and suffering from the trauma she had sustained. He imagined he could hear her desperate pleas for help, as Cavallaro continued to beat and assault her. And, he remembered gazing at her burning home realizing her body was being destroyed as he watched.

Bartlett now realized he should have been more concerned about Moira, at least, until after they were back in St. Croix. She would have been much safer in the Virgin Islands than in the States. His trip to Los Angeles was a mistake, and he now realized it should have been postponed until after his business affairs in Detroit had been concluded.

Bartlett's tendency to pay close attention to detail was

one of his strengths; on the other hand, predictability was one of his weaknesses.

He had made the trip to Los Angeles to purposely take care of one of those ancillary details. An associate hit man, he had employed at times, needed to be eliminated. Bartlett had utilized the man's services for years, and they enjoyed an acceptable working relationship. Bill Morgan knew more about John Moore, and his mode-of-operation, than any other living human being. When Bartlett decided to retire, he knew the elimination of all loose ends, including Morgan, would be a priority. After his return to Evanston, from California, Bartlett quickly realized that getting rid of Morgan was the right call but at the wrong time.

Morgan was pleased by Moore's unexpected phone call that he was visiting Los Angeles and wanted to get together for dinner. Morgan was anticipating a meeting to discuss another one of Moore's lucrative business opportunities. Instead, he found himself being attacked by Moore outside his rural home. When Morgan approached his garage, Moore quickly appeared and fired two bullets, at close range, into his head. Morgan collapsed instantly. The .22 caliber pistol had been equipped with a suppressor to deaden the sound. Bartlett was assured there would not be any witnesses, due to the fact Morgan lived alone in a desolate area, several miles outside of town.

He recalled how he had loaded Morgan's body into the bed of his awaiting pick-up truck 40 feet from the kill site. He rolled the corpse into a blue plastic tarp and headed to a nearby canyon where he buried the body.

He had thought about the possibility of Ricci eventually hiring Morgan to kill him. Bartlett knew he could not trust Morgan, or anyone else, when it came to business. He felt justified in killing Morgan whether he was a long-time associate or not.

Bartlett concluded his business at a Wells Fargo bank in Los Angeles where he stored an ample amount of get away cash. He placed the bills in a leather briefcase and headed for the airport to return to Chicago. It was late in the evening when Bartlett got back to Evanston. He never anticipated, or was prepared, for the tragedy awaiting him inside Moira's home.

* * *

Bartlett loved his coastal house high atop the hills on St. Croix. He knew he would miss the panoramic ocean views, the continual tropical breezes, and the sounds of the surf below. He wished he did not have to leave the island. However, he understood he had no other choice if he wanted to protect himself. If they could find him in Evanston, Bartlett knew he could be found anywhere. Moving and relocating was the smart thing to do.

He got out of bed and checked the clock. It was almost six o'clock when Bartlett opened the front door and went out onto the porch. Drinking a cup of coffee, he enjoyed the view along with the early morning breeze. As he sipped the drink, Bartlett thought again about his future plans for Cavallaro, Ricci, and Wallace.

Several days later, Bartlett was sitting at his desk, where he had been most of the day, when Rosa quietly appeared in his doorway. She looked like she had something to say. "I've locked the doors, made the deposit, and cleaned the display cases Mr. Bartlett," she said. "Is now a good time to talk?"

"Sure, you can ask me anything," he said.

"I've reviewed the materials you gave me, and I have several questions," she said.

"Ask away," Bartlett said.

"If you want things to remain a secret concerning our partnership, I'm fine with it. But, what if something were to happen to you? How would I be able to prove my ownership rights?"

"Once we agree on the partnership, I will have my attorney prepare a document stating you as the owner and me as your silent partner. The document will include a schedule on when and how ownership changes may occur. Essentially Rosa, you will be the owner from day one and I will be like a stake holder in your company, like your banker. As long as you continue to pay me off according to the terms, everything will be fine. If you fail to pay me, then I will have an option to either buy you out or renegotiate the terms. Does that make sense to you?"

"Yes, I think so. What if I want to pay you off earlier? Could I do that?"

"Yes, the schedule sets up the terms and you could pay

me off early without any penalty. It will be stated in the contract," Bartlett said.

"Okay. If I understand you correctly, you will still receive your share of the profits based on your ownership percentage, which will be decreasing every time I make a monthly payment to you. Also, part of my profits will include the money I would be saving from your former salary in the shop."

"Yes, exactly right," said Bartlett.

"Why are you giving me this opportunity? I still don't understand. No one has ever treated me like this before."

"There are several reasons. First, I trust you, and I like you. You have been very loyal to me, and because of these things I want to help you have a better life. Besides, I don't need to work in the shop anymore. But, I still want to receive a monthly payment, kind of like a small pension. As you probably have assumed, I have other sources of income and I want to concentrate more on those larger ventures. I don't need, or even want, to sell the shop at the moment, but it gives me a reason to return to St. Croix, from time to time."

"How will I pay you?"

"Does your question mean you accept my offer? If so, congratulations," he said.

"Yes, it does. Thank you so much," she said, as she hugged and kissed him very affectionately. Bartlett noted she was more aggressive than he.

"I'm happy for you," Bartlett said, as he hugged and

kissed her in return. "I'll go ahead and proceed with the details."

"Sounds perfect," she said.

He imagined there were fire crackers going off in her head because she was so excited. At that moment, Rosa's beauty and sensuality seemed so apparent and available to him. He wondered if her meaningful hug and kiss were meant as a thank you or unconsciously as an invitation. Was she offering herself to him, Bartlett wondered. He had been lusting after her for a long time and maybe now, he might be willing to accept her invitation. However, Bartlett knew mixing business with pleasure was generally not a good idea, but loneliness had weakened him several times before.

* * *

Back in Detroit, Ricci had arranged to meet Minello for dinner at Sal's Italian Restaurant, on the northwest side of town. When Minello arrived he found Ricci sitting alone in a secluded booth. After dinner Ricci said to him, "I've been thinking about modifying our plan on how we approach Ms. Parker. Instead of getting tough right away, I want you to contact her as if you were looking to hire an attorney to represent you in a legal matter. Introduce yourself under a fictitious name. Tell her it's urgent you meet tomorrow evening because you are going to be out of town for the next several weeks. Suggest a dinner meeting at Lisa's Place, which is a charming little restaurant in Parker's neighborhood. Reserve one of their obscure, outside tables for dinner. Wear a nice business suit, and buy her a good meal. Be cordial and friendly."

"Okay, then what do you want me to do?"

"Tell her you want to hire her to handle a legal matter for you. Hand her an envelope with $10,000 in cash, and tell her there is more coming if she does as you ask."

"Okay," Minello said. "Then what?"

"You will have her immediate attention when she sees the cash and she will know you are a serious person. Tell her you need her to retrieve some important documents that Henry Wallace had illegally taken from you. She will probably tell you he is her client and that she won't be able to help you. That's your key to hand her the other envelope with the photographs of her son. When she sees the photographs, Ms. Parker will know that someone has been watching him for the last several days."

"What else do you want me to say?"

"Nothing. She will be confused and probably frightened. She'll understand you are a very dangerous and serious person. Just tell her you'll be in touch with her in the morning, get up, pay the check, and leave the restaurant."

"Aren't you worried she'll tell Wallace or the authorities?"

"She's not stupid, and you didn't really threaten her in any way. You just showed her some photographs of her son and nothing more. All you are asking her to do is represent you in this matter. She'll be very worried about the photos and I'd imagine she will proceed very cautiously. Besides, she doesn't know who you represent, and the bogus personal information you gave her will shield your identity. The next day call her at home before she takes the kid to school, and ask if she is going to help you or not. Remind her of the benefits of working together, and tell her there are risks if she does not. Don't be specific about the risks. Understand? We've got nothing to lose here and everything to gain."

"But Dominic, aren't there more risks associated with this strategy than with our previous plan?" questioned Minello.

"Yes, there are, but we can always have our men get tough with her later on, if she chooses not to cooperate. Besides, the kid should be our wild card with her," Ricci said.

"You're probably right."

"Have our guys bugged her phones yet?" asked Ricci.

"I'm not sure if they've finished, but we've been working on it. I'll let you know when things are in place."

"Okay, I'll see you tomorrow morning at the office," said Ricci."

Chapter 17

Rosa Rodriguez awoke at five-thirty, in her shabby rental home, located outside of Frederiksted on the western side of the island. Many of the wealthier properties on St. Croix were closer to Christiansted on the eastern side overlooking the Caribbean shore.

Rosa smiled as she looked at herself in the mirror. She wanted to look really good as she applied the finishing touches on her make-up, and again combed her thick, long black hair. She still couldn't believe her good fortune regarding the shop.

I'm going to own my own business.

Although Rosa was elated with the opportunity Bartlett had given her, she was saddened by the thought of losing him. Secretly, she had been hoping for months for an opportunity for them to be together. Rosa felt Bartlett had always been kind, sweet, and gentle to her. Occasionally, she wondered what it would be like to be married to him.

Rosa had been married only once before to her late husband, Juan Rodriguez. When they first got married Juan had demonstrated some good qualities, but she hadn't thought of him as a good man for quite a long time. She had been in love with him, but because of his criminal involvement, regular drug use, abusive nature, and incessant adultery, their relationship had suffered. In reality, she had begun to dislike him. Just before his death, Rosa knew she was no longer in love with him, and that she wanted him out of her life forever.

However, Rosa was impressed and excited by Bartlett's good looks, glorious physique, and seemingly good character. For months after she had started working at The Ursula Shop, she had dreamt, more than once, about kissing and romantically touching Bartlett. Sometimes, she had even fantasized about making love to him, regardless of her marital status.

When Juan had unexpectedly disappeared, she knew her marital status would no longer be a problem, particularly once his partially decomposed corpse had been found. Rosa realized she was finally free to pursue Bartlett, or anyone else, once a respectable time had passed.

Rosa had always been able to help support her family by working hard at a variety of legitimate occupations, but her deceased husband was the exact opposite of her. Juan had always chosen crime. In Puerto Rico, he had been involved in the drug trade, first as a runner and later as a low-level drug pusher. When he got caught by a drug dealer, attempting to take more than his share of the profits, Juan was viciously attacked but somehow survived. His poor judgment had forced them into fleeing Puerto Rico, and all Rosa's relatives, for their own protection. A few days later, he and Rosa arrived in St. Croix, intending to start a new life. At least that's what Juan had promised her.

However, once in St. Croix, Juan quickly acquired another drug related job, in spite of Rosa's constant pleas for him to seek a legitimate opportunity, like working at the local oil refinery. Two months later, according to the word on the street, he had been trading drugs for sexual favors from several local married women. The police report speculated that he might have been killed by one of the disgruntled husbands. It was apparent, looking at his remains, that he had been pummeled and stabbed numerous times, indicative of a crime of passion. The authorities were still trying to determine who was responsible for his death, but nobody was talking.

At one point, the police questioned Rosa about a possible connection between her and Juan's death. However, the authorities were unable to find concrete evidence against her, and eventually she was dropped as a suspect. Months passed without resolution, and the police finally decided to close the case.

Outwardly Rosa seemed very upset, but inwardly she was relieved that Juan was finally gone. Everyone knew Juan was not a good person, but they had no idea how difficult he had made Rosa's life. Few people were really saddened by Juan's fate, and privately, most thought she was better off without him.

Her only regret was that Juan was no longer there to provide income, and occasional companionship.

Thankfully, Bartlett's proposition would make it easier for her to have a more secure and happy life.

When they sealed the deal in his office, Rosa recalled how she had tried to act rather modestly as she hugged and kissed Bartlett. Consciously, she knew she had been more aggressive than she probably should have been, to the point that her actions could have been perceived almost lovingly. At that moment, she remembered feeling excited and slightly aroused. She hoped Bartlett had felt something special for her too.

Rosa wondered if now would be a good time for them to get together, since his relationship with Moira had obviously changed. She had sensed that Bartlett was not as detached as she would have imagined. Maybe that was why he did not want to talk in more detail about his motives. However, some things about the arrangement, and Moira, still did not make sense, she thought.

If Moira were out of the picture totally, I'd have a better chance to be with him.

Realizing she was going to be late for work, Rosa stopped pondering about Bartlett and hurried to catch the bus to Christiansted. She did not want to be late, particularly if Bartlett was in town. She realized she would have to work harder than ever to make their partnership successful.

Early in the afternoon, Bartlett emerged from his office and approached Rosa. "I need to make a short business trip to Puerto Rico. I'll only be gone for a few days," he announced. "You haven't scheduled any time off, have you?"

Surprised that he had considered her schedule, Rosa responded, "No, Mr. Bartlett. I'll be here. Go ahead and take care of your business."

"I thought I should tell you more about my plans, since we're going to be partners," he said.

"I appreciate your consideration, but it's not necessary. I'll always think of you as my boss, until I have paid off my debt."

"Alright," said Bartlett. "Anyway, I need to meet with my attorney in San Juan to initiate the documents pertaining to our arrangements. I won't be gone very long. It'll probably only take me a few days."

"Okay, I'll see you when you get back," said Rosa.

* * *

The following afternoon Bartlett arrived in the Cayman Islands, following a brief stop in Puerto Rico. He was promptly met outside the airport terminal by an attractive blond named Sandra White. She was holding up a small sign with his name written on it. After a brief introduction, the pair got into her red BMW convertible and headed towards town. Ms. White was a local real estate agent, whom Bartlett had contacted to show him property. She suggested they have lunch at a waterfront restaurant, favored by the locals. After some casual conversation,

Bartlett began talking to her about his reason for the visit.

"Ms. White, as I told you on the phone, I am technically in transition until my home sells in the States. I am a semi-retired business owner. I'd like a place to continue my on-going work, and to pursue a retirement writing project. I am very interested in looking at a secluded hideaway to rent for right now. It doesn't have to be the nicest property on the island, but it has to be clean and private. I am anticipating my house will take six months to sell, so I want to rent on a month by month basis. However, I'd be willing to pay six months in advance. How many properties do you have to show me?"

"Well, after we talked last week, I located several properties I'd like you to see. Also, I've booked a room for your stay at a friend of mine's bed and breakfast. I think you will be quite comfortable there. We can start looking at properties this afternoon, or we can wait until tomorrow. Whatever your preference," she stated.

"This afternoon would be preferable," he said.

"Okay, we'll get started after we eat our lunch."

"That sounds great. I need to conclude my business here as soon as possible."

"I understand," said Sandra.

* * *

Back in Detroit, Sammie Parker had a restless night

following her brief evening meeting with Mr. Joseph Vertucci, who had requested her legal assistance. He had given her a $10,000 cash retainer, and alarmingly, had provided her with some photos of her son, Kevin. Parker was having a cup of coffee, contemplating her response to Vertucci, when the telephone rang.

Sammie let the phone ring several times before she answered. "Hello," she said.

"Ms. Parker, this is Joseph Vertucci calling. Did you enjoy dinner?"

"Yes, I did," she said. "Thank you."

"Since we are both very busy people Ms. Parker, I'll skip the pleasantries and get right to the point. Are you interested in helping me or not?"

"Well, I am curious about what exactly you want me to do. You already know Mr. Wallace is a client of mine, and as such, it would be a conflict of interest if I were to work for you. You certainly understand that don't you?"

"Yes, but this is a very important matter, and to be quite frank, you were especially selected because of your relationship with Henry Wallace. You would be very well paid for your assistance. My associates are very serious-minded people, who can be trusted to be discreet. We know how to treat our friends and how to treat our adversaries. If you need more time to think about our request I can give you …"

"I don't need more time," Sammie interrupted. "I'll do it but I'd like to know some specifics."

"What do you want to know?"

"Well, for starters, who do you really represent?"

"I work for a holding company that encompasses a dozen or so corporations, owned by several parties. My bosses wish to remain anonymous but the holding company name is Breakaway Properties Limited. Wallace has documents associated with Breakaway that he obtained illegally and my associates want them back."

"Alright, if I understand you, my only task would be to help you get back the documents in Mr. Wallace's possession. Is that correct?"

"Yes. You would need to acquire the documents and return them to me."

"How would you propose I do that?"

"That's up to you, and why we are willing to pay you so handsomely for your assistance."

"Well, what if I was to decline your offer or I'm unable to help you?"

"There are always choices and consequences for our actions Ms. Parker."

"It appears I have few choices. That's why I'm going to do it," she said. "However, I have a request for you too. No, think of it as a condition of employment," she stated.

"What else do you want from us?"

"You keep my son out of this matter, or you'll never get those documents from Wallace. Do you follow me?"

"I'm glad you've decided to help us Ms. Parker. No problem about the boy. That is, if you do your job."

"Give me a few days, and I'll call you with an update."

"That's fine but I'm going abroad. I'll have to contact you myself. By the way, I meant to tell you last evening that you have a lovely son. I'm sure you're very attached to him," he said.

"Yes, I am. Thank you," Sammie said, sounding remarkably unshaken and in control, despite the implied threat.

"Goodbye Ms. Parker. I'm so glad you've made the right choice," said Vertucci, as he abruptly hung up the phone.

"Goodbye to you too asshole," Sammie mouthed back, after she heard the phone click. She was almost certain who Mr. Joseph Vertucci represented. Breakaway probably belonged to Dominic Ricci and members of the Detroit Partnership.

"How stupid do they think I am?"

Almost immediately, she had imagined it was Ricci who was behind Vertucci, trying to pressure her into getting the documents back from Wallace. Wallace had vaguely talked to her about them. No doubt they were what Wallace had on Ricci, and why he felt he would be temporally safe.

For the immediate future, Sammie understood dealing with her current situation would be her number one priority. She'd have to consult with Wallace, as soon as possible, because she knew Ricci wanted his documents back, and he would do anything to get them. She realized she was in a very awkward and dangerous position, because of her association with Wallace. She didn't like it, and that was the reason she had agreed to help Vertucci. Even though she despised and feared Ricci, and the mob, she'd have to figure out a way to work with them, and still maintain Wallace's safety and her own.

Chapter 18

Grosse Pointe, Michigan is an upscale coastal suburban city, bordering Detroit, Michigan. On its northeastern border is Lake St. Clair. Gross Pointe is recognized by its historic reputation for having glorious scenery and landscaping, architecturally magnificent homes and buildings, and having an east coast like atmosphere.

In the previous century, Grosse Pointe was home to cottages, resorts, farms, and widely spaced lakefront mansions.

Gross Pointe Shores is a prestigious area known for its extremely wealthy citizenry, and among other things, the Gross Point Yacht Club. Wallace's property is located on Lake St. Clair, not very far from the Yacht Club. The residence is a stately and modernized Colonial style home, sitting on a large, well-manicured, sprawling lot. Wallace's morning ritual always included sitting in his wood-paneled office, drinking coffee, and reading the Detroit Free Press. Outside, the glimmering sunshine on the lake, always looked very serene in the summertime. He wondered how long he would continue to enjoy those views, before one of Ricci's men came to kill him.

No reason to worry right now, he thought. What's done is done. I've got some time left because Ricci still thinks he needs me. However, it won't be too long before I have to figure a way to ensure my safety and permanently neutralize him.

It was eight-thirty when the telephone rang in his office. He picked up the receiver and was pleasantly surprised to hear the voice of Sammie Parker on the line. "Henry, we need to talk, and very soon," she said, sounding emphatically resolute. "Something has come up, and I really need your help."

"What's going on? Do you want me to come there, or can we meet somewhere else?" asked Wallace, sounding concerned.

"I'm calling you from a pay phone inside the Thompson Hotel in Birmingham. I am probably being watched, and my phones are surely either bugged or soon will be," she said. "I will have to contact you like this in the future. I'm sorry that I am acting so paranoid, but you never know what to expect from thugs."

"What thugs?" asked Wallace.

"I'll tell you more when I see you," she said. "Can we meet after lunch?"

"Yes, certainly we can. How about meeting me at the Detroit Institute of Art at two?"

"Okay, I'll be at the van Gogh exhibit in the Dutch

galleries on the third floor," said Sammie.

"I'll meet you there," said Wallace. "There are plenty of quiet areas within the exhibits where we can sit and talk privately."

"Thank you Henry. I'll meet you there."

* * *

Back in the Cayman's, Bartlett was planning to return to St. Croix early Friday afternoon, just in time for the weekend. Fortunately, with the help of Sandra White, he had been able to find the perfect setup for himself. He had rented a very secluded, single-bedroom, newly renovated home, located on the eastern side of the island. The rental was not on the water but was hidden by overgrown vegetation, and a quarter mile away from Queens Highway, one of the main roads on the island.

He was glad White had been able to help him find the property and interested as to why she had told him about her recent divorce at lunch. Bartlett believed she was temporarily seeking an emotional connection, and he was always ready to accommodate a vulnerable and very attractive woman. Later that evening, Bartlett was pleased to have been given the opportunity to console her and become her lover for the evening. Ms. White turned out to be an exceptionally good lover. So much so, that Bartlett wanted to spend more time with her. Sandra was older than Bartlett but had proven to be physically capable, energetic, and willing to have a totally sexual relationship with him.

Once he moved to the Cayman Islands, Bartlett had plans to welcome Sandra into his bedroom on a regular basis.

* * *

After the plane landed back in St. Croix, Bartlett hurried through customs, retrieved his bag, and drove directly to the shop. Rosa was pleased to see him back and gave him a smile after he entered the shop. "How was your trip?" she asked.

"Everything went as planned," Bartlett said. "After you lock the door tonight, please come back to the office and I'll tell you all about it."

"Alright," Rosa said, again smiling pleasantly.

Just after closing at five o'clock, Rosa appeared at the office door and asked, "May I come in and sit down?"

"Yes, sit," he said. "But before we get started, I want you to start calling me Jim instead of Mr. Bartlett. Mr. Bartlett seems far too formal for partners, don't you agree?"

"Well, I guess so," she said, blushing.

"I have good things to report. My attorney will be sending all the paperwork in a couple of days, and everything is arranged as we agreed. Once we sign the documents the business will be yours. Your first payment will be due on the first of every month. You can send your check to an investment account I have established in the Cayman Islands. I will provide you with a copy of all the details as soon as I receive them. Do you have any questions?"

"No, I think you have explained everything very clearly. I just want to thank you again. I can't tell you how very excited I am."

"I'm very thankful for you, and I am excited for you as well," said Bartlett. "This is kind of a spur-of-the-moment thing, but I would like it very much if you would join me for dinner tomorrow evening. That is if you are free, of course? I'd like to celebrate the beginning of our new partnership. What do you say?"

"Oh Mr. Bartlett … uh sorry … I meant to say Jim," she said, smiling innocently, and feeling slightly embarrassed. "I would be very happy to have dinner with you, to celebrate our partnership."

"Great," said Bartlett. "Do you want to meet me somewhere for dinner, or should I pick you up at your home?"

"Are we going to be having dinner in Christiansted or do you want to go somewhere else?" asked Rosa.

"It's your choice, but I think it makes more sense to dine somewhere in Frederiksted than elsewhere, since you live nearby. Can you pick a nice upscale place in town because I'm not as familiar with the restaurants there?"

"Sure, there are several nice places to eat along the

shore. I'll make a seven-thirty reservation at one of them, and I'll be ready to go by seven," she said.

"That sounds great to me. I'll be at your house at seven, that is if you give me directions. I don't know where you live," he said, sounding playfully cheerful.

"No problem," she said. After a minute, Rosa handed him a piece of paper with her address and a small map for him to follow. "It's easy to find," she said. "You'll see. I don't have many neighbors."

I can't believe he's finally asking me out. I wonder what this means, she thought, feeling excited and confused, as if she were a young girl. Is this really about business, or is it something else? I guess I'll find out Saturday night.

* * *

Back in Detroit, outside the Thompson Hotel, sitting in a non-descript, white Ford van, Minello's men waited patiently for Sammie to return. She had parked along the street, across from the hotel, and had quickly gone inside. Sammie had come to the Thompson directly after dropping her son off at St. Jude's school.

The mobsters wondered whether she was there for a breakfast meeting or visiting a guest in the hotel. They had no idea how long she would be, so they decided to eat a biscotti with their morning coffee.

Surprisingly, she spent only five minutes inside the

hotel before returning to her Mercedes. They followed her again as she sped away from the hotel and headed towards the Interstate. Traffic was heavy, so they only allowed four or five cars between them. They assumed she was going downtown to her office or to one of the Court buildings.

At one-thirty, Sammie reappeared, got back into her car, and drove directly to the Interstate. Several miles later, she pulled off the roadway and headed towards the Detroit Art Institute parking lot, just off Woodward, in midtown Detroit.

The men debated about following her inside, but they were concerned they might look out of place in the museum. They had miscommunicated that morning and were both dressed like workmen. They agreed at least one of them should have been dressed more business-like. Reluctantly, they decided to stay in the van and wait for her to return.

Sammie hurried from her Mercedes into the museum and headed directly for the elevators and the third floor. She was a frequent visitor to the Art Institute and knew exactly where to find the Vincent van Gogh exhibit.

When she arrived at the Dutch galleries, she noticed that Wallace was looking at van Gogh's oil on canvas painting, entitled "Portrait of Postman Roulin" reported to be valued in the $80 to $120 million range. Upon hearing the sound of high heels, Wallace turned and spotted her immediately. He signaled for her to come join him. "I can't believe how much this painting is worth," he said.

"It's unique I suppose," she said, looking at the

painting. "But this one is not my favorite painting from his body of work."

"I agree," said Wallace. "But what do I know. I was able to find a secluded area over this way where we can talk. What's this about anyway?" he asked, as they walked to the alcove. "Does this have something to do with Ricci?"

"Yes it does. You are very perceptive."

"Why thank you. I've apparently learned something in my 40+ year's legal career. But getting back to you, I've never seen you quite this worked up before. What's going on?"

"I met a potential client last evening at a Birmingham restaurant, by the name of Joseph Vertucci. Do you know him?"

"No, never heard of him," said Wallace.

"He wants me to help him retrieve some documents pertaining to Breakaway Properties Limited that you supposedly have in your possession. He said you obtained them illegally."

"Alright, go on."

"He handed me an envelope with $10,000 in cash, which he said was a retainer, and indicated there would be more coming, if I agreed to help him retrieve the documents from you. He wouldn't tell me who he was working for, but I quickly decided it was Ricci."

"I wouldn't be surprised if Paul Minello is your Mr.

Vertucci. He's Ricci's top guy. Ricci trusts him like a brother. I'd say he is one of the more accomplished and polished mobsters that I've met in the Ricci organization."

"I don't know. I've never met, or been involved with either one of them," she said.

"So, what's the problem?"

"Not only did he hand me the cash, he also handed me several pictures of my son Kevin, at school. And, Mr. Vertucci commented about how attached he thought I might be to my son."

"Alright, did he say anything else?"

"Yes, he referred to how they know how to treat their friends, and enemies too. And, he implied there would be consequences for me, if they didn't get what they wanted from you."

"Did you contact the authorities?"

"Hell no!" she said. "These guys are ruthless, and I'm not going to risk putting my son's life in jeopardy over our relationship. I need to figure a way out of this mess so nothing bad happens to either one of us. Do you have any ideas counselor?"

"Yes, maybe I do. So glad you didn't call the police. I know Ricci has some of the higher-ups on his payroll. Let me think about it for a while. Go look at the exhibits, and come back here in about a half hour. I should have something figured out by then. Between the two of us we are a lot smarter than they ever thought of being. Try to relax Samantha; we'll come up with something."

Thirty minutes later, Sammie returned to the partitioned space, and found Wallace scribbling notes on several pieces of paper. "Did you figure it out?" she asked.

"Yes, I think I did. It's very simple. If I give you a copy of the Breakaway stuff, and you give it to Vertucci, or whomever, that will satisfy your responsibility to them. Based on what you've told me, that's all they said they wanted, right?"

"Yes," said Sammie.

"When they examine the documents they will realize how damaging they would be if they got into the wrong hands."

"Okay but if you give me their documents they will assume you no longer have anything on them, and then they will kill you."

"No, you tell them I gave you a copy but I had another one made too. Tell them I stored it in a bank safety deposit box, and there is no way you can get hold of it. Tell them I never revealed the name of the bank to you. And you tell them that if anything potentially harmful befalls my family, I will see to it that the Prosecutor gets the Breakaway documents immediately."

"That's not going to help me very much. They're probably going to threaten me and Kevin even more then."

"What can they do to you?"

"Abduct my son. Beat the crap out of me or worse, torture me," she said, excitably.

"Think about this Samantha. Explain to them that upon my death those Breakaway documents will be in my safety deposit box with instructions to be turned over to the Wayne County Prosecutor. If you're dead, you won't have access to the box any longer. But, if you are alive, as my executor, when the county deputy auditor opens the box for tax purposes, you will be there to retrieve the documents. However, if you are deceased, your responsibilities as my executor will pass to the bank's trustee, who will become my executor. Do you see where I'm going with this?"

"Yes, I certainly do. It's brilliant."

"I will change my will to delete my family members as my executor, and name you and the bank as co-executors. Therefore, if we are both deceased those documents will go into the hands of the authorities, and the Riccis will be screwed."

"However, if you are alive you can take the documents out of the lockbox and assure the deputy auditor you will be turning them over to the Persecutor but instead you will give them back to the Riccis. It's as simple as that. There it is. You and I, and our families, are all protected."

"You should also remind Mr. Vertucci that I am 72 years old and in poor health. I'm not going to live forever. If they are willing to be smart, and patient, they will ultimately get the other copy of their documents back too."

"You're a genius Henry," she said.

"No, I'm just a really smart lawyer, and so are you. You

would have figured it out sooner or later."

"Now wait, what keeps them from killing you right away to get the documents back immediately?" Sammie asked.

"Nothing," said Wallace. "You know if I'm not under the witness protection program, I could be killed almost any day, right?"

"Yes, but I thought you weren't going to testify. Have you changed your mind again?"

"No, I haven't."

"Okay, so if you don't testify, eventually you will be charged with several crimes and probably be convicted, and have to go to jail."

"Exactly. That's why I have to totally disappear right away," said Wallace. "If I'm not dead, or cannot be proven to be dead, my lockbox will stay unopened at the bank; unless the prosecutor wants to legally take possession of it. I doubt if they would do it though, because first they'd have to find the bank."

"That shouldn't be a problem for them, should it?" questioned Sammie.

"Well Samantha, you decide. The lockbox is in an obscure, little farm town community bank in northern Michigan. I've had the box a long time, and I used a now deceased, former buddy's hunting lodge mailing address on my application. Remember, things were much simpler then. There were not nearly as many regulations as there are now. The bank has no idea where I actually live or who

I am. They just have my name in their little 4X6 filing card system, which they have used for years to keep track of their box holders. I always paid for the box with cashier's checks from various banks, but during the last ten years I paid with cash. Last year I purposely decided to pay them in advance for ten more years. Anyway, I'll send you the particulars, including the bank's location and my official last will and testament, before I leave. In the event of my death, you will be notified, and you will have everything you need to settle my affairs."

"Sounds like you've given this a lot of thought."

"I've had lots of time to think since this whole mess blew up. I should have never gotten involved with Ricci, but I did it for the money. They paid me more than handsomely, and for many years. Over time, I got involved in the family businesses too. Anyway, I will be free to live my life outside of the country, fairly soon. God knows I have the money to hide for a long time."

"But, you'll never be able to see your family again?"

"No, but that's the price I'm willing to pay for my mistakes and poor judgment."

"Sad. Where will you go?"

"Not sure yet, but I'll never tell you, unless you want to be an accessory by knowing my whereabouts."

"No thanks Henry."

"Please do me one favor.

"What do you need?" she asked.

"I need at least three days to finalize my plans, before I can leave. If you could wait until early next week before you tell Mr. Vertucci anything, I would appreciate it."

"I'll wait. Good luck Henry," Sammie said, as she leaned over and kissed him on the cheek. "I'm going to miss you," she said.

"As I will you," Wallace said. "Goodbye Samantha. Don't worry, everything is going to be fine."

Chapter 19

Bartlett had not dressed up for dinner on the island in a long time. Normally, Rosa only saw him wearing khaki shorts and a colored T-shirt in the shop. He had selected his favorite sport coat, and a light blue dress shirt to wear on the date. Before he left the bathroom, he splashed some cologne on his face and admired himself in the mirror. Bartlett liked his look and hoped to make a good impression on her.

Saturday evening at six-fifteen, Bartlett pulled out of his driveway and sped towards Frederiksted. He wondered about the date, as he drove to Rosa's house,

Why am I doing this? I still care about Moira, but I have needs too, he thought. Under the circumstances, I wonder if she would object to me moving on so quickly with my life. I'm the only one who will ever know anything about tonight, he reminded himself. I'll see how the evening goes and what happens. Maybe things won't be as good with Rosa, as I've always imagined.

Several minutes before seven o'clock, Bartlett pulled

up to her home. He wasn't surprised to see the house was in poor repair. In fact, he kind of expected it. The outside was very weathered, but she had obviously attempted to make the yard and the sparse amount of landscaping look presentable.

Bartlett approached the front door and knocked several times. Rosa immediately appeared, and he was stunned by her overall appearance and natural beauty. Her long black hair was glistening in the doorway along with the alluring scent of her perfume. She wore a beautiful red, black, and white halter-top dress and beige heels. The dress highlighted her curves in all the right places, and her dark-complected skin perfectly contrasted with the colors in the dress. She had manicured finger and toe nails, and she had selected the same deep red color for her lips, as well. Bartlett could hardly believe his eyes.

What a knockout, he thought. I have always found her to be an attractive woman, but she really looks marvelous tonight.

For several seconds, he stood and gazed at her shape, before finally responding. "You look gorgeous," he said.

"Thank you Jim, you look very nice too. We've got a few more minutes before we have to leave. Would you like to come in for a drink?"

"Sure. What've you got?"

"Well, I have chardonnay, or I can make you something with rum. Which one would you like?"

"Rum sounds good," he said. "Are you drinking?"

"No, I'll wait until dinner," she said.

Ten minutes later, Bartlett assisted Rosa into the Jeep and they headed north towards the luxurious Sunset Beach Resort Hotel and Spa. Inside the resort was The Crucian Room, which was an expensive gourmet restaurant that overlooked a beautiful sandy beach. The Crucian offered epicurean-quality dining with an upscale ambiance. Their menu varied depending on the local catch, but the restaurant featured prime meats, chicken, pasta dishes, several jazzy Crucian traditional meals, and a variety of fresh seafood.

"When the couple arrived at the restaurant, Rosa asked, "Have you ever eaten here before Jim?"

"No, I didn't know this place even existed because I usually eat somewhere closer to Christiansted. I guess I should have expanded my horizons before now. It really looks nice. Have you been here before?" he asked.

"No but I have always wanted to," she said. "I hope it's not too expensive."

"Don't worry I can afford it."

The maître d' quickly showed them to a beachfront table after Rosa told them she had a reservation. Once they were seated, a waiter appeared with menus and a wine list, and offered them either Perrier or tap water to drink.

When the waiter left, Bartlett asked Rosa, "What looks good on the menu?"

"Everything, but I want to try something different. I've never had a filet mignon before. Are they good?"

"Yes, dry-aged prime beef is usually very good. I'm sure you'll love it. Do you like champagne?"

"I've only had it a couple of times at weddings. It was pretty fizzy and bubbly but it tasted very mild and refreshing. I liked it."

"Let's get a bottle," he said.

The waiter quickly came back when he saw Bartlett motion for him. "Would you please bring us a bottle of Dom Perignon," he said.

"Certainly sir, right away," said the waiter.

Several minutes passed and the man returned with a bottle and two glasses. "Would you like me to pour for you sir?" asked the waiter.

"Yes," Bartlett said, "that would be fine."

When he had finished drinking his glass of champagne, Bartlett quickly refilled both of their glasses. Several minutes later, the waiter reappeared and took their dinner order. When he left, Bartlett invited Rosa to raise her glass and offered a toast. "All the best, to one of the most deserving and beautiful ladies I have ever had the pleasure to be with," he said. "My hope is our partnership will do well, and prosper for many years."

"Here's to lots of profits," she said, as they playfully clicked their glasses together. And thank you Jim, for the nice compliment," she said, smiling brightly, as she looked favorably at him.

"You know you're very deserving of my praise Rosa."

"I'm flattered with your remarks and I will try my best to be a very good partner. Again, thank you so much for this evening and for your confidence in me," she said, as she leaned over and surprised him with an appreciative kiss. "I am so excited about this opportunity. Really, I don't know how I could have been any luckier in my life. I'll always be grateful, and I hope you will never regret your decision," said Rosa. Several tears appeared on her cheeks after she had spoken.

"Hey, this is a happy occasion," Bartlett said, when he noticed tear drops running down her cheeks. "If you're going to be so serious you'll mess up your makeup. This is a night for us to have fun and celebrate. The seriousness, and the work, will resume on Monday morning. Tonight, let's just relax and enjoy the evening."

"Here's to a great time," she said, as she raised her glass again. It was apparent to Bartlett that she was already feeling the effects of the champagne.

Jim is really a very special person. I'd like to hug and kiss him again but I'm afraid he might object. Maybe I'll try later, she thought.

After the entrées were served, and the couple had eaten several bites, the waiter returned and asked if everything had met their expectations.

"Yes, everything is delicious," said Bartlett.

"Very good, sir," the waiter said. "If you need anything else, please let me know. Also, if you are interested, our resort band will be playing dance music starting at nine. They will be out on the veranda and, of course, you're welcome to stay."

"Thanks, we'll check it out after we've had our dinner," Bartlett said.

"If the music is good, could we dance for a while?" asked Rosa.

"Sure, I'll dance, but I must warn you, I'm not the greatest dancer," he said.

"That's alright, I'm pretty good at it," she said, confidently. "I'm certain we'll be just fine."

"How's your filet?"

"Everything is really delicious," she said.

"Good, I'm glad you liked it. While we wait for our desserts, please finish telling me about your family."

"Oh, alright. My father was Puerto Rican and my mother was Italian. They both worked at the Roosevelt Roads Naval Station in Ceiba, Puerto Rico, during the 50's, 60's, and 70's. According to my Mom, when she was introduced to my Dad, it was love at first sight. They got married soon after they met, and my oldest sister was born less than a year later, on July 11, 1953."

"How many siblings do you have?"

"I had three, two sisters and a younger brother but he died from lung cancer several years ago."

"Oh, I'm sorry," Bartlett said.

"He had been a long-time smoker."

"Who did you get your beautiful black hair and those

enticingly gorgeous blue eyes from? Was it your Mom?"

"Yes, she was a very beautiful woman," said Rosa, who was feeling very appreciative, surprised, and slightly aroused by his compliment.

"Are your parents still living in Puerto Rico?"

"No, they were both killed in a car accident when I was ten years old. My grandmother raised me until I turned 18. I moved out on my own after graduating from high school."

"Is she still alive?"

"Yes, she's an amazing woman. She'll be 90 on her next birthday. I just love her. Are your parents still living Jim?"

"No, they passed away a long time ago. My father passed first and then my mother."

"I'm very sorry," she said. "Do you have any siblings?"

"I had a younger brother, but he died years ago too. Hey, enough about my family. You're out of champagne. Should I pour you another glass?"

"Not for me. I've already had too much to drink. Are you going to be okay to drive?"

"Yes, my tolerance for alcohol is pretty high, particularly on a full stomach. I'll get us home safely. I might have one more drink before we leave but that will be it," he said. "The music is about to start. Do you want to dance?"

"Sure, I'd love to. Besides, I think I need to move

around a little bit, it might help sober me up," she said, grinning.

"Don't worry about it, you're fine. We'll dance for a while and then go back to your house, alright?"

"Sure, I love to dance," she said, almost slurring her words.

I didn't realize that she was this close to being drunk. She must not be as big a drinker as I would have presumed. I'd better cut her off before she passes out on me, he thought.

Bartlett was glad the band was playing mostly romantic songs. He thought slow dancing with her would stimulate her feelings for romance, later in the evening. When the band started playing one of his favorite songs, "Always and Forever," Bartlett held her a little more tightly, and softly caressed her back with his other hand. When they took a short break from the dance floor, Bartlett could hardly take his eyes off of her. She was a stunning woman and he recognized that he wanted her now, more than ever.

They danced another half-hour, sharing some delightful moments amidst the slow and rhythmically romantic sounds, until the band took their first break. "Are you having a good time?" Bartlett asked, when they sat down to rest.

"Yes, the music is really good and you aren't that bad of a dancer either," she said, smiling. "I drank a little too much champagne tonight. I feel like I might be drunk and I'm tired. Would you mind if we went home?"

"No, that is fine. I'm starting to get tired myself and I have more than an hour's drive, from here to your house and then home."

"Are you sure you are alright to drive? You've had quite a lot to drink," Rosa inquired.

"I'm fine. I ate plenty of food, and I'm almost twice your size. Besides, I'm used to drinking more than you."

"Jim, I'm sorry I am being so overly cautious, but I'm always kind of afraid in these situations. My parent's accident occurred because of alcohol."

"Rosa, don't worry. I am a long way from being unable to drive. I will be very careful. Trust me," he said. "I won't let anything bad happen to you."

Bartlett remembered making the same pledge to Moira, and reminded himself what had happened to her. He decided to drive over-cautiously for Rosa's benefit. When they got to his Jeep, he wondered if he should try to reassure her again that everything would be fine. Fortunately, once he started the engine and got underway, it appeared she was comfortable with his driving. They had a pleasant conversation and she was enjoying the drive back to her home.

When they arrived at Rosa's house, Bartlett walked her to the door, gave her an affectionate hug and a romantic kiss, and decided it would be wise to say goodnight. He turned, intending to leave, when he heard Rosa say "Why don't you come in for a drink?"

"I thought you were worried about my drinking?" he

said, seemingly puzzled by her question.

"I am, and that's why I want you to spend the night with me," she said. "I don't want anything bad to happen to you. Please, come hold me again."

Bartlett turned and walked back to her. He held her more firmly this time, gave her a very sensuous kiss as he slowly caressed her body, and lightly began touching her breasts. She responded quickly to his kiss and touch, and their emotions erupted into a frenzy of passion at the front door. Recognizing what appeared inevitable; he hurriedly took her inside, laid her on the living room couch, and made love to her.

Afterwards, while they were still lying on the sofa, locked in a romantic embrace, Rosa said, "If I told you that I'm in love with you, would you be surprised?"

Bartlett responded, "Lately I've wondered, more than once, about some of the gestures you've made towards me. Were they gestures of gratitude, or were they hints that you were attracted to me? To answer your question, no I'm not totally surprised. But, are you sure our love-making this evening wasn't just about the alcohol," he asked.

"No, it's not the alcohol," she said, softly. "I've had these feelings for a long time. I know you are still involved with Moira, but I decided to tell you anyway, because I thought I might never get another chance. I really want us to be together."

"I'm very thankful, but you really don't know me on a personal basis yet. As I've told you before, Moira and I are not as close as we once were but I haven't forgotten about her either. If we were together you wouldn't want to share me with her, would you?"

"No but it is not my decision to make. If you want me, I'm here for you. I want to be your lover, your companion, and your best friend."

Why am I even thinking about not taking her up on her offer? My God, he thought. She is a knockout and a very passionate lover. I'm quite surprised because I always thought of her as being the innocent type. Man was I wrong! Besides, Moira is dead. Hell, why not? I'm not planning on getting married anytime soon. I can't think of a good reason not to get to know her better. If we're together for a while, and I like being with her, I could change my mind about marriage.

Bartlett hesitated briefly, looked into her blue eyes and said, "I don't ever want to hurt you and I don't want to hurt Moira either. Unfortunately, somebody is going to get hurt if we take this much further. To tell you the truth, I have been thinking about ending my relationship with Moira."

"I won't be hurt," she said. "I just want an opportunity to show you how much I care for you."

"Rosa, I am willing to end my relationship with Moira, but I don't want you to think that what just happened tonight, even though it was wonderful, will lead to marriage, or anything else. I'm concerned, if our relationship doesn't work out, for whatever reason, we could damage our business agreement. For right now, we don't know each other well enough to be anything more than just special friends. But believe me; I am definitely very attracted to you and interested in being with you. So, if you want to be with me, let's give it a try. Is that okay for now?"

"I'm fine with it, as long as you promise to end your relationship with Moira, and as soon as possible. Otherwise, there's no chance for us to be together. I would never consider sharing you with another woman."

"I promise. I'll end my relationship with her, but give me a little time," said Bartlett, pleading his case.

"Fair enough," she said, as she embraced him very passionately again. And, after another sensuous and romantic kiss, she said, invitingly, "If you want to make love again, my bedroom is right back there. The mattress is more comfortable than the couch," she said, smiling convincingly at him and pointing back toward her bedroom.

Bartlett watched as she quickly arose, removed her remaining clothing, and got into bed. After a few seconds passed, Bartlett got up and joined her.

Chapter 20

Just before sunrise the following morning, Bartlett awoke and made love to Rosa again. Around ten, while Bartlett showered, she got up and started making breakfast. She was more than satisfied with the outcome of the weekend. Not only had she become the new owner of the shop, but she had begun a serious relationship with Bartlett too.

With a smile on his face, Bartlett walked into the kitchen. "Something smells good," he said, as he approached her at the sink. She turned and put her arms around him and gave him a passionate kiss.

"Good morning honey," she said. "How'd you sleep?"

"Like a baby," he said. "It's been a while since I've slept that good. I really like your bed. I guess I'm going to have to spend more time in it," he said, smiling at her.

What a wonderful lover, she thought. He's an older man, but still a very capable and passionate lover.

Pausing briefly, she replied, "That's fine with me but

somebody has to get up to go to work. Unlike you, I'm not retired yet. I have a boss who wants his monthly payment," she said, jokingly.

"Gosh, he sounds demanding. I bet he's really a great guy, if you get to know him," said Bartlett.

"Oh believe me, I intend to get to know him well," she said. "In fact, I think I already have a good idea about what he likes," she said, teasingly.

"Yeah, I think you have too," he said, smiling. Is breakfast ready yet? I've worked up quite an appetite."

"I'm just waiting on you," she said, kissing him again. "What do you want to do today?"

"Well, maybe go shopping or we could go to the beach. But, it's your day off too," he stated. "What do you want to do?"

"I just want us to be together. We don't have to do anything but stay here and enjoy each other's company," Rosa said, with an enticingly playful look on her face.

"Sounds great but sometime this afternoon, I want to go shopping at the Sunshine Mall. I want to buy you a gift."

"What are you going to buy me?"

"Something nice, maybe a piece of jewelry to commemorate our first weekend together," he said. "That way you will always think of me when you wear it."

"That's really sweet but you don't have to buy me anything. I will remember you, and the weekend, believe me," she said.

"I know I don't have to buy you anything, but I want too. Is that okay?"

"Yes it's fine and very nice too," she said, as she gave him another kiss. "I'd be very appreciative of anything you gave me."

* * *

It had been a hectic Monday morning for Parker in the Wayne Co. Circuit Court. Sammie had made three appearances for clients and she was ready to go back to her office. When she arrived, her secretary informed her that a Mr. Vertucci had called several times asking to speak to her.

"Did he leave a message?" she asked.

"Yes, but only that he'd call back later."

Just before five o'clock, Sammie heard the telephone ring and her secretary say, "Yes, she's here. I'll connect you."

Seconds later, her telephone rang and Sammie picked up the receiver. "Samantha Parker," she said, sounding very official.

"Ms. Parker, this is Joseph Vertucci. Have you made any progress?"

"Yes, I think so," she said. "I spoke with Wallace this afternoon and to my surprise; he told me he had some important documents that he wanted me to keep for him, as a precaution, in case something bad ever happened to him or his family."

"Did you tell him about our arrangement?"

"No. Why would I do that?"

"You tell me."

"Look, I phoned him today under the guise of discussing some strategies that I've been working on for his defense. During our conversation, he informed me about the documents," she said. "Does that satisfy you?"

"And, you never mentioned to him our conversation?"

"No, I did not," she said, emphatically.

"Did he identify what information was in the documents?"

"No, he only said they were important. And, he told me not to open the envelope because he didn't want me to be involved."

"When did he say he would be giving you the documents?"

"I'm to meet him on Wednesday morning in the lobby of Comerica Bank in downtown Detroit. I'm presuming they are the documents that you want. I'd guess they're in his lock box."

"Ms. Parker, here's what I want you to do, when you receive the envelope, verify if the documents belong to us or not, and give me a call. I'll send someone to pick them up."

"What if Wallace wants the envelope back after I've given it to you?"

"Don't worry he won't need it any longer. Once the contents have been reviewed, you will receive the balance of your retainer. Thanks for your help," he said, as he hung up the phone.

No, thank you Mr. Vertucci, Sammie thought. You are going to be very surprised and upset when you receive the documents and I tell you more about my conversation with Wallace.

* * *

Wednesday morning Sammie arrived at Comerica Bank and was not surprised to see Wallace waiting for her in the lobby. "Hi Samantha. Are you ready?"

"Yes, I talked to Vertucci on the telephone late Monday afternoon. He didn't act surprised when I told him you wanted me to hold the documents for safe keeping. He also has no idea that I am fully aware those documents pertain to Breakaway Properties."

"Very good Samantha," said Wallace. "Let's go to the vault and retrieve the envelope that I have prepared for you."

"Alright," she said. "Incidentally, Vertucci instructed me to verify if the documents were his before he would send someone to pick them up. I didn't mention to him that you told me the contents of the envelope were copies and not the originals."

"Good," he said. "I'm certain Vertucci and Ricci will be very angry when they find that out, but I am hoping they will be patient enough not to do anything stupid. They should know the consequences."

"Yes, I'm sure they don't want those documents getting into the wrong hands," she said.

"You've thought of everything, haven't you Henry?"

"I sure hope I have," said Wallace. "Your involvement with them should end when they receive their documents and when they learn you will no longer be in touch with me. At least I'm hoping it works out that way."

"I'm sure it will Henry. Take care of yourself and good luck."

* * *

Wednesday afternoon Sammie called the telephone number Vertucci had instructed her to call. The phone rang several times before a taped message began to play. The message was, "Leave your information, and your phone number, in case we need to contact you again."

After the beep, Sammie left the following message:

Good afternoon Mr. Vertucci. This is Samantha Parker calling. I have an envelope containing the Breakaway documents ready for you to pick-up. Therefore, as far as

I'm concerned, my arrangement with you has been fulfilled. No further monies will ever be requested or required, and I have enclosed a reimbursement check of $10,000, inside the envelope, for you.

You should know that when I talked with Wallace at the bank this morning, he told me that the contents of the envelope contained only copies and that there was another set of identical documents stored elsewhere.

He told me that due to his up-and-coming legal problems, his age, and his poor health, that he was going to disappear permanently, following our meeting. For everyone's protection, he told me he would no longer be in touch with me, or any member of his family.

However, he instructed me to remind you that he would turn over the other set of documents to the authorities, if anything bad ever happened to me, or his family.

Also, he informed me that he had appointed me, and Comerica Bank, as his co-executors, in place of his family members. He gave me a letter instructing me to handle all his affairs upon his death.

As Mr. Wallace's attorney, I can assure you that you will ultimately be receiving the other set of the Breakaway documents back, as per my client's instructions, as long as you continue to abide by the arrangements you agreed to.

However, I hope you realize, in my absence, the bank would be in charge of settling his estate, and I'd have no control over what might happen to your documents.

Therefore, I do not feel there is any further need for us to communicate until I am notified of Mr. Wallace's death.

Chapter 21

Early Thursday morning, Bartlett awoke, rolled over in bed, and briefly gazed at Rosa's figure as she slept. He thought about making love to her again but decided to let her sleep.

What a gorgeous woman, he thought. Apparently, ever since her husband's death, and maybe before, she had been a very vulnerable and horny woman. I could have been making love to her long before now. Rosa probably would have been my girlfriend, if I hadn't been involved with Moira. At the time, all I could think about was Moira, I was in love with her and we were going to be married. I couldn't envision myself ever being emotionally involved with another woman. Obviously, my outlook changed with Moira's death. Nonetheless, I wonder if it is necessary to change my career, after all. I doubt if I'll ever get as emotionally attached to anyone, as I was to Moira.

Bartlett strolled into the bathroom, and was standing at the sink, when he felt Rosa's hand lightly caressing his back. "Couldn't you sleep?" she asked.

"No, I just woke up to go to the bathroom."

"Are you coming back to bed?" she asked inquisitively.

"Nah, I'm awake now and not very tired. I thought about reading for a little while before I go back to bed."

"You might want to reconsider," she said, with a playful smile on her face. "I was dreaming we were making love again when you got up. Want to do it for real?" Rosa said, naughtily.

"That sounds nice."

"Get back into bed honey; I'll be in after I wash up," she said.

At seven o'clock the alarm went off. Bartlett awoke and quickly rolled out of bed. He could smell the distinct scent of bacon cooking in the house. A few seconds later, he appeared in the kitchen wearing only his briefs and a t-shirt. He was pleasantly surprised to see Rosa wearing only a short silk robe and panties. When Rosa leaned forward to turn over the bacon, Bartlett watched as the tan lines on her buttocks appeared. "What a nice view," he commented.

"I think I'm spoiling you too much."

"I don't think so. You are a very sexy woman, and I appreciate your femininity."

"Don't expect this every day," Rosa said teasing him.

"No, I won't," Bartlett said. "But, how about a repeat performance tomorrow morning?" he said, chuckling with a sly grin.

"Well, I'll see how nice you are to me."

"I'm always very nice," he said.

"I know you are," said Rosa laughingly. "I'll see what I can do."

"Sounds fair," he said. "Incidentally, you'll be pleased to know, I'm planning on going to Chicago on Saturday. Can you get along without me for a while? I need to go see Moira and break up with her, as I promised I would do. Afterwards, I need to be in Miami for a business meeting the following Monday."

"I can manage," she said, trying to be as relaxed as possible. But, emotionally, she was extremely excited about Bartlett moving so quickly to break it off with Moira. "Thank you darling," she said, as she hugged and kissed him romantically. "When you're gone, I miss you way too much, but under the circumstances it's fine."

"I know you were expecting the Chicago trip, but not the Miami business meeting. For now, I don't have much of a choice. I'll make it up to you later. I promise."

"I'm sure you will, but I hate it when you're gone."

"For now, that's the way it's got to be. Things will get better," promised Bartlett.

"If things go as expected, I should be back by the following weekend, but I'll keep you posted. Okay?"

"That's fine. I understand you have things that need to be taken care of. Let's eat and get ready for work. Hopefully we will be busy today, because the cruise ships start arriving in Frederiksted around nine."

"How could I forget?" said Bartlett. "Have I ever told you about how I found out about St. Croix?"

"No, you didn't. Tell me," she replied.

"A long time ago I took a Caribbean cruise out of Miami, where the ship made a stop in St. Croix. After visiting for several days, I realized I really liked it there. That's when I decided to return, build a house, and start a business. The rest is history," he said.

"I guess it was lucky for me that you decided to take a cruise, or we may never have met."

"Yes, you're right, but I was also there on business," Bartlett said, regretting the comment right after he'd made it.

"Really, what kind of business were you on?"

"Nothing interesting," he said, trying to cover up his obvious error. "We better get ready or else we're going to be late for work."

"Okay, but promise me you'll tell me more about your life, in the not so distant future," requested Rosa.

"Sure, I will," said Bartlett, trying to sound believable. "You can count on it."

I remember the cruise alright, he thought. I was given a contract by the Chicago mob. A trusted executive, from one of their Las Vegas properties, had retired with mob money he was not supposed to have kept. He thought he had fooled them, but they eventually found out and I was contracted to kill him. I threw him overboard in the middle of the ocean, two days after we left port. His girlfriend did not miss him until the next morning. She mistakenly thought he had been in the casino gambling for most of the night.

* * *

Thursday evening, at Ricci's rural Michigan home, Minello and Don Ricci are sitting in his den discussing Parker's message, and the ramifications of Wallace's decision. "What do you think about this situation with Wallace? Should we be content to wait it out and trust that Wallace will not try to double-cross us again?" Ricci asked Minello.

"Well, I'm not a lawyer, but I'd say he has made it almost impossible for us to do anything to him, his family, or Parker's. I'm surprised I'm saying this but I think we are going to have to wait and trust him, despite how we feel about it."

"What about the criminal charges that have been filed against me? Do you think the prosecutor can convict me without Wallace's testimony to corroborate the hit man's story?"

"What does your attorney say?"

"He claims if Wallace doesn't testify against me, it will make my case much easier to win. However, as you know, anything can happen in a jury trial. Senator Stroh is going to testify that Wallace approached him to gain support for the casino bill. Also, he'll say Wallace had indicated to him, at the business meeting in Holland, he was there representing me."

"What do you think?" asked Minello.

"I'm concerned. I don't have the confidence in Rosenfeld that I had in Wallace."

"He's your attorney now Dominic, and supposedly, a very brilliant lawyer too. You should trust him. However, whatever happens to you will affect all of us. Most of the captains are getting concerned about all the heat this trial is putting on their business interests. They can't understand why this situation wasn't handled differently. They're surprised that Wallace and Stroh are still alive. If things are not taken care of pretty soon, we could have some disgruntled and worried crew members on our hands."

"I'm sure they are worried, but it shouldn't be a problem for them."

"Why not?" asked Minello.

"Because I'm the one under indictment for those charges, not them," said Ricci.

"Maybe they're afraid you might involve them too."

"You mean rat on them?

"Yes," said Minello.

"They don't have to worry about that, but if they don't start earning better, I might have to make some changes the captains wouldn't like," said Ricci. Frankly, I think they are more scared of you than me. That's one of the reasons I made you my underboss," said Ricci.

"They're probably not going to be that much of a problem. I'll talk to the captains and explain what's going on. Between the two of us, I think we can handle them. On the other hand, I'd be very happy to take care of it for you, if necessary."

"Okay, you handle it. I'm sure everything will work out with the men. However, right now I'm more concerned about Ms. Parker. I don't trust her. I doubt if she's telling us everything she knows. At this point, maybe I should have Tony put his gun down her throat and make her an offer she'd be wise not to refuse," said Ricci.

"What good would that do?" asked Minello.

"She might know where Wallace is hiding and how we could get those damn documents back."

"Dominic, I don't know if that is such a good idea. If she decided not to talk, we'd have to go through with our threat. She could be more useful to us alive than dead."

"Yeah, I suppose you're right. I'm glad you're with me Paul. You keep me from letting my emotions get us into trouble. In the old days, Stroh, Wallace, and Parker would already be dead, regardless of the consequences. Anymore, I wish we could go back to doing things like we used to do. It was much simpler to make a buck then."

"Unfortunately Dominic, we can't go back. The Partnership has had to change over time and the authorities are trying harder now days to make it more difficult for us to do business."

"Yeah, I know. I will not be able to run this family forever. Paul, I think of you as part of my family. When I step down, I'll see to it that you're the next boss. Right now, just do what you can to help me get through this mess."

"I'll help you Dominic. You know I always do what is best for you and the Partnership," said Minello.

"Thanks for your respect and loyalty; it means a lot to me, and I won't forget it," Ricci said, as he arose and hugged his underboss. "Now, let's go to the kitchen and eat," he said. "My wife just made a fresh pot of gravy with braciole and sausage. It's my favorite dish and she only makes it on special occasions, like birthdays and holidays, or when I request it," Ricci said, appreciatively with a bright smile.

* * *

Sunday morning, Rosa was home watching television when her telephone rang. She answered the call and was pleased to hear Bartlett say, "I miss you honey. How are you getting along without me?"

"I miss you too baby. I was getting worried because I hadn't heard from you since you left for the Mainland. Where are you? Is everything alright?"

"Things are going as I expected. I just wanted to call and tell you I talked with Moira and told her I wanted to end our relationship, and I was no longer interested in getting married. That comment pretty much ended our conversation and the relationship. She was extremely hurt and upset but reluctantly agreed to us splitting up. It was a very hard couple of days. But, ever since you and I've been together, I've realized I made the right choice."

"Darling, it must have been a very stressful situation for you, and I'm sorry. I appreciate the fact that you have chosen to be with me. My intention is to make sure you never regret leaving Moira to be with me. You have no idea how much I love you and appreciate being with you."

"I'm glad to hear that you love me and want us to be together. I want the same, even though it was very hard for me to have to hurt Moira. I'm convinced she'll eventually get over me and move on with her life."

"I'm sure she will," proclaimed Rosa. "I understand it's still hard when relationships end, but life goes on. Hey, where are you now?" Rosa said, changing the subject.

"I just arrived in Miami. I barely have enough time to prepare for my business meeting. It's possible that I may need to be in town a little longer than I had anticipated, but I'll try my best to be back for the weekend."

"It's alright if you have to stay longer. Do what you have to do, and I'll see you whenever you get home. I love you," she said.

"I love you too," Bartlett responded.

Chapter 22

Monday afternoon, Bartlett arrived at O'Hare International Airport, via a direct flight from the Cayman Islands. He had spent a delightful two days there, having sex, and touring the island, with his new friend, Sandra White.

He rented a compact car near the airport and began the six-hour drive to Detroit, Michigan. Bartlett had chosen to fly into Chicago rather than Detroit, in an effort to conceal his presence in the Detroit area. Besides, he thought the drive would afford him more time to think about his plans for Tony Cavallaro and Dominic Ricci. After driving three hours, Bartlett stopped to eat at a roadside restaurant, near Battle Creek. After eating a large meal, he rented a room at the Holiday Inn and retired for the evening.

Bartlett was glad that his dreams about Moira were almost completely gone. Lately, he was expecting to dream about his more familiar wartime experiences. As he crawled into bed, he hoped to sleep soundly and free from the interruptions of nightmares. However, around two in the morning, Bartlett awoke with beads of sweat dripping from his face. Apparently, his thoughts had drifted from the quiet and peaceful environment inside the hotel room, to an incident that had occurred during the Vietnam War.

Awake, he instinctively looked around the room for an enemy and after seeing none, quickly began to rehash the dream. He could almost recite it by heart, because it had been with him for almost three decades. The dream was like an unwelcome relative who keeps reappearing at family functions, whether they are invited or not.

It was fall 1968, near the Demilitarized Zone. The platoon was fifty-miles northwest from their Army base near Da Nang. His eight-man squadron was climbing a dangerous mountain path. They were headed for sector Alpha, listed on the platoon map. The prior day's patrol had been uneventful and they had not come upon a single North Vietnamese Army soldier. Bartkowski was relieved because encounters with the NVA generally resulted in injuries and casualties, to his soldiers. The squadron was already short two men from the prior week's operation, and replacements were not expected anytime soon.

Sergeant Bartkowski was in his second tour of duty in-country. He had been assigned to fight the Viet Cong during his first tour of duty in the south, and during his second tour, he had been reassigned to fight the NVA in the north.

In the north, the trails through the mountainous regions were steep, overgrown with vegetation, and treacherous, with a variety of insects, snakes, small and large animals, and booby-traps.

Gary Mishler was on point and John Bartkowski was in the middle of the squadron. The men had been humping it up a steep hill for half an hour with back packs, weapons, and ammunition.

Bartkowski gave the signal for Mishler to stop and for the squadron to spread out for a quick break. Things were quiet except for the sounds of birds and small animals moving on the hillside. No NVA appeared to be nearby.

The men in the squadron were already fatigued, tired, and vulnerable. The torrid morning sun, and the humidity on the hillside, were extremely harsh on the men. Their uniforms were almost totally soaked with sweat. The soldiers were glad for the short break; several smoked, opened C-rations, and all of them drank water from their canteens.

Mishler in the front, and Jimmy Miller in the rear, they watched, and listened, for any sign of an approaching enemy. They detected none. After five minutes, Bartkowski signaled the men to get up and resume the climb.

The orders for day two of the current mission were to sweep the middle of sector Alpha. All four squads in the platoon were involved in the operation.

The platoon lieutenant hoped his troops would be able to locate, engage, and kill as many NVA as possible. At headquarters, the commanding general was ratcheting up the importance for increased enemy body counts, no matter what the cost.

Bartkowski calculated another forty-five minutes of climbing before the squad would arrive at their destination. Along the way, he was hopeful they would not encounter an ambush.

Fifteen minutes after resuming the climb, Bartkowski told Stevie Jackson to relieve Mishler on point. Jackson was one of the least experienced men in the squadron. Bartkowski decided to move up behind him, in case anything happened. He had trained Mishler for point and he was training Jackson too. He always told his soldiers to watch out for trip wires, tunnels, and booby-traps.

Five minutes later, Jackson's foot unfortunately snagged a trip wire, causing a grenade to roll towards them. It stopped five feet from their position and the two men instantly stared at the grenade, expecting to be either seriously injured or killed from the blast.

Instinctively, Bartkowski yelled, "Grenade! Hit the deck!" Several seconds passed and the rest of the squadron dropped to the ground, trying to shield themselves. To everyone's shock and surprise, the grenade failed to detonate. Grenade traps were common and often encased in discarded, United States military, C-ration cans. When Jackson tripped the wire, the grenade came out of the can, its handle was supposed to open and cause the explosion. Apparently, the device had been there for a long time and the handle had rusted on the grenade, not allowing it to detonate. Jackson looked over at Bartkowski, who appeared to be extremely upset, and said, "I'm sorry Sergeant. I almost got us killed!"

Bartkowski ignored him and immediately said, "Let's get the hell out of here before the God damn thing goes off. Mishler you're back on point. Be careful, there may be *other booby-traps here that work."* The squadron quickly moved past the grenade and continued up the trail.

Bartkowski knew they had been extremely fortunate and lucky. The grenade could have killed or injured them both. *I'm keeping Mishler on point until I feel more comfortable trusting the other men,* he thought.

Unfortunately, after reliving the dream, Bartlett was wide awake and unable to go back to sleep. It had been a while since that dream had surfaced, but he was sure it had unconsciously reappeared, because he was preparing to enter a war zone again.

His mission was to find, interrogate, torture, and eventually kill Tony Cavallaro. Bartlett's plan included the elimination of Cavallaro first before dealing with Ricci.

Bartlett imagined Ricci had ordered his men to interrogate Moira. He was convinced that once the interrogation began, Ricci would expect her to be weak, vulnerable, and very loose lipped.

He was surprised and shocked that Cavallaro had molested and mortally wounded Moira. He could not believe a supposedly shrewd mob boss, like Ricci, would knowingly sanction such a thing, particularly to an anonymous contract killer's girlfriend. It did not make any sense to him.

* * *

Late Monday evening, Tony Cavallaro returned to his rural Livonia residence and pulled his Cadillac into the garage. He had spent most of the day with his girlfriend; eating, watching television, and having sex. Minello had called him earlier that afternoon and had outlined a busy schedule for the following day. He was tired and ready to go to bed.

Cavallaro unlocked his back door, went inside, and was reaching for the light switch when he received a hard blow to the back of his head. The mobster collapsed on the floor and was out cold. Several minutes later, he awoke to the smell of an ammonia strip that was placed under his nose. When he awoke it was dark, and he quickly realized he was blindfolded and firmly secured to a wooden chair.

"Does this remind you of anything Tony?" a voice stated from behind.

"No. Should it?"

"I thought you might remember. Oh, and I took the liberty of removing your Tiger's commemorative bat from the case. I hope you don't mind that I hit you with it. I tried not to damage the bat."

"Who the hell are you and what do you want?" said Cavallaro, nervously trying to see who was talking behind him.

"I'll bet the back of your neck really hurts, doesn't it?"

"What do you think asshole?"

"Don't you recognize my voice Tony? I'm the guy who cut off your finger in Saugatuck, Michigan, a while back.

As it turned out, I should have slit your throat instead of letting you live."

"What do you want from me?" Cavallaro asked anxiously.

"We'll get to that a little later but first were going to play your favorite sport. I've been admiring all your Detroit Tigers memorabilia. Your collection is quite impressive."

"What kind of game, you sick bastard?"

"Baseball. Batter up Tony. Oh, I'm sorry you aren't free to use a bat right now. I'll swing for you."

Seconds later Cavallaro felt a hard blow to his chest, as Bartlett hit him right below his windpipe. Tony grimaced with pain when the bat hit its mark. "Are you fucking crazy?" he shouted in pain. "Do you realize who I work for?"

"Yes. I know everything I need to know about you."

Within seconds Cavallaro took another blow from the bat, this time in his groin area. The sensation was so painful, Cavallaro almost passed out.

"Damn Tony, judging from your response, that looked awfully painful. Sorry! Okay, we'll call the first swing a strike but that last one was definitely a ball, wasn't it?" Bartlett said, seemingly amused by watching Cavallaro suffering. "Count is one and one. Want me to continue, or do you want to talk to me?"

"Why are you doing this to me?" questioned Cavallaro,

who was about to speak again, when he felt a powerful blow to his abdomen. "God!" he yelled, feeling the sharp pain and hearing the sound of his ribs fracturing inside his body.

"Ouch! I imagine that one hurt too, didn't it?" By this point, Cavallaro was in so much pain, he was beginning to shake and sweat profusely. "I'm sorry, I'm not really all that great as a hitter. I've been practicing ever since I arrived," said Bartlett. "Let's see, the count is two strikes and one ball. What do you say we talk Tony? Why did you molest my girlfriend? Are you some kind of sexual maniac?"

"What are you talking about? I didn't do anything to your girlfriend," Cavallaro lied.

"You tell me who did then!"

"It was my partner who did all the rough stuff. I was there, and I tried to get him to stop, but he wouldn't."

"What's the guy's name?" demanded Bartlett.

"Parisi, Jimmy Parisi. He's the one who assaulted your girlfriend, not me. I tried to help her, I swear," said Cavallaro, lying again about the incident.

"Tony, I know you're lying. Before she died, she told me you were the one who assaulted her. Hey, I think I just heard the umpire yell, play ball. Didn't you? Okay then, batter up."

"No, wait! I did it to her but I didn't intend to kill her. I was just trying to scare her into talking."

"Where do I find Ricci and how can I get to him?" asked Bartlett.

"He lives on a large estate, an hour north of Detroit, near Lake Orion, but he has body guards and the compound is secured with fencing and attack dogs."

"How many body guards?"

"Five, maybe more, and they are heavily armed."

"Where is he most vulnerable?"

"I don't know. He hardly leaves the compound anymore, except when he goes to the city to screw his Canadian whore."

"Where do they meet?"

"Dearborn, I think. I've never gone with him. He has a helicopter that takes him into the city. I'm only his cousin, but Paul Minello, his underboss, knows a lot more about his schedule than I do."

"Is there anything else you can tell me before we get the game started again?" asked Bartlett.

"I've told you everything I know. Are you going to let me live?

"I've been thinking about it, but first it's time to finish the ball game. Batter up."

"Hey man, I'm really sorry about your girlfriend; I was just trying to do my job," Cavallaro said, almost sobbing.

"Sorry isn't gonna cut it. She's dead. It's my turn at bat again. I'm going to try to hit a home run this time."

"Wait! Wait!" shouted Cavallaro, as the bat was about to strike him firmly in the center of his head. "What can I do …" Cavallaro was saying, as the bat impacted his skull. When it hit, particles of flesh and blood splattered all over the room. Within seconds, Cavallaro's body began to convulse and shake, just before his head slumped to the side. Bartlett reached over and checked his pulse. There was none. "Strike three," he pronounced. "You're out of here," he said, as if he were an umpire. One down and one to go, he thought, as he dropped the bat and left Cavallaro's home.

* * *

The village of Lake Orion is a quaint, historic, lakeside community located in northern Oakland County, approximately 45 minutes north of Detroit.

Dominic Ricci resided, ten minutes from Lake Orion, in a 12,500 square-foot mansion located on 50 acres of prime farm land. Ricci's compound included a small lake, a large forest, and fertile grazing land for his stable of horses. He employed two full-time servants to tend to the household chores and several workers, who took care of the stables and the grounds. Currently, at least five of his men were there to protect him, and his wife, from any of his potential enemies. Lately, Ricci had not left the residence, since his troubles began with the authorities. However, unbeknownst to his ailing spouse, he would occasionally visit his girlfriend, from Windsor, for sex and companionship.

* * *

Late Tuesday morning, Minello picked up the phone and called Cavallaro. The telephone rang several times before Minello decided that Cavallaro was either not there or was unable to answer the call. Cavallaro was supposed to meet him at the office for a business matter, but he was already two hours late. Minello disliked Cavallaro but had always found him to be prompt and ready for an assignment. A half hour later, Minello called Parisi and asked him to go check on Cavallaro.

Thirty-minutes later, Parisi called to inform Minello that he had found Cavallaro's body at home, duct-taped to a chair, and indicated he had been plummeted to death. Immediately, he assumed the hit man had paid Cavallaro a visit. He called Ricci to inform him about Cavallaro's death.

"Dominic, Parisi just called me," Minello said. "I think our hit man is in town. He told me he found Tony at home, bludgeoned to death. What do you want me to do?"

"My helicopter is in the hanger at the airport. Bring more men to the lake house. I think we're going to need them."

"Okay, I'll make a few calls and have them there in a couple hours. I doubt if he would try anything during the day but I guess you'd be more vulnerable at night. What do you want me to do about Tony? Should I call the authorities?"

"No. Tell Parisi to clean up the mess. Put Tony on the couch and torch the home. Tell him I want it to look like an accident. I don't want the cops nosing around into our affairs more than they already are."

"Okay, I'll take care of it Dominic. I'll have five more guys at your house tonight. I'll be at the Surplus store in case you need anything."

"Okay," Ricci said, appreciatively, as he hung up the phone.

* * *

Ten minutes later, Minello called Corrado De Luca, one of the five captains in the Ricci family most affected by the negative aspects of Don Ricci's legal troubles. "Corrado, we need to finish our conversation about the Don from the other day. Can you talk?"

"Sure, what's on your mind Paul?"

"You remember when we were talking about business and how we've all been suffering over the last several years?"

"Yeah."

"I just talked to Ricci and he wants five more men at the lake house for protection. If you count the five already there, the three at the hanger, and the others at the Surplus store, we are dedicating a dozen or so men just to protect Ricci's ass. The hit man took out Cavallaro sometime Monday night, and I'm sure he'll try to kill Ricci next."

"Okay, what do you want me to do?"

"Before I ask you for anything, I have a question for you. How do you and the other captains feel about the Don?"

"They like the old man but they think he's weak and isn't as shrewd as he used to be. The captains are worried he might rat if he gets convicted on those charges," said De Luca. "But, don't tell him I ever said that."

"I like the old man too, but he isn't helping the Partnership anymore. He's got several of our best earners on security details. Recently, he told me he longs for the old days and finds it harder to do business now, than ever before. And, he said if business doesn't improve pretty soon, he'll be forced to make some changes the captains won't like. He is definitely slipping. I don't think he'd ever betray us but why take the chance. Would your guys support me for Boss, if I made a move against the Don?"

"Are you shitting me? You can't kill a Boss without approval from the Commission," De Luca said, nervously.

"Yeah, I know, but what if the Commission thought he was killed by a rouge and disgruntled hit man, who had been threatening him."

"If the Commission ever found out the truth it would be very bad for you Paul. They wouldn't hesitate to put a contract on you."

"I know but who's going to tell them? Are you?" Minello asked, with a stern look on his face.

"Hey Paul, I'd never rat you out," said De Luca, cautiously. "We go back a long way."

"Yeah we do …" Minello stated. "Alright then, I guess there isn't a problem. Do I have enough support to be voted in as the Don's replacement?"

"I can't speak for the rest of the Captains, but I wouldn't have a problem with it. We're all tired of kicking up more money to him and having to save his ass again. Anyway, the Captains don't want to worry about getting more heat from the police investigators. Ricci really fucked up by trying to kill that State Senator."

"Yeah, I know. I tried to tell him but he wouldn't listen," Minello said, emphatically.

"How would you do it?"

"I'll kill him myself and frame the hit man. I figure I'd only have to kill Ricci, and maybe a guard or two, to make it appear believable. What do you think?"

"It sounds feasible. I think you're right. It could work. With Cavallaro out of the picture, it might be the perfect time."

"Corrado, I'll make you my Underboss, if I can count on you to keep quiet about the hit and if you support me for Boss. The pay and influence are much better than being a Captain, I assure you."

"You have my support and my word that I'll keep quiet

about this matter. When will you do it?"

"I'll have to do it tonight. I'm going to postpone sending more men to the house until tomorrow morning," said Minello.

"If you need anything else, give me a call. But, I'm going to be very busy all night creating a solid alibi for myself," said De Luca.

"Whatever, go ahead and do what you have to do, but don't try to contact me either; I'll contact you when it's done," said Minello.

Chapter 23

Around noon on Tuesday, the gate guard at the Ricci estate noticed a dark-colored pickup truck slowly approaching from the south. He wondered who the driver was, who had waved to him as he passed by the guard shack.

Probably a local farmer admiring our place, thought the guard. I know the locals are generally more friendly than people from the city.

After thinking about it for a few seconds, the guard sat down and resumed his mid-morning nap.

Bartlett had located the estate without any trouble and thought he could easily access the property, either in the early morning hours or late at night. He assumed Ricci had already been told about Cavallaro's death. Bartlett was surprised the guard had not appeared too interested in his presence there.

The expansiveness of the estate was not too troubling for Bartlett. In fact, he thought it might be helpful. The mansion sat far off the highway, and the large horse barn was not far from it. The small lake and dense woods were nearby too. The property was well maintained, and Bartlett assumed he could easily hide in the woods, and quickly gain access to the barn without being detected. As he passed the property, Bartlett could hear the sounds of dogs barking in the distance. He assumed they were there for the mobster's protection.

Continuing down the road, Bartlett made the decision to visit Ricci later that evening. He had dealt with dangerous scenarios before. His visit would not be a total surprise but he had one advantage; the moon was waning and his mission would be carried out in almost total darkness. He figured, if everything went well, he could do the job in about half an hour and be on his way back to the Interstate. Moira's death would be avenged and he could go back to St. Croix, satisfied that he had killed those parties responsible for her death.

* * *

Eight o'clock Tuesday evening, Minello pulled his black Cadillac into the driveway of Ricci's estate and stopped at the guard shack. The guard immediately recognized him and opened the gate to let him pass. Several seconds elapsed, then he stopped next to the shack and signaled for the guard to come over. "Hey, where is the other guy? I don't see him here," Minello commented, gruffly.

"He's at the house Paul. The Don pulled him off gate duty about an hour ago. He's with the other men outside in the yard. I'm glad you're here Paul; somebody else should be inside with the Don. Supposedly, he is allowing only one guard inside the house. We heard about Cavallaro. I guess the hit man got to him already. We figure Don Ricci might be next."

"I'll take care of the Don," Minello thought, as he pulled out a .22 caliber pistol with a silencer, and shot the guard twice in the head. Immediately the guard fell to the ground. Quickly Minello got out of the car, dragged the dead man behind the gate shack, closed the gate, and raced towards the mansion.

The home was more than a quarter mile from the front gate, and Minello sped rapidly towards it. He could see the outlines of the men standing outside, as he approached. He wondered why the grounds were dark. The Cadillac was almost air-borne before it came to a screeching halt.

Minello emerged from the vehicle, as the men ran towards the car with guns drawn, ready for action. "The guard is not at the front gate, and the gate was wide open," he said. "Have you heard anything? Why aren't the floods on?" yelled Minello frantically.

"Don Ricci came outside, several hours ago, and told us to turn the floods off," explained one of the guards to Minello.

"The killer is here on the estate right now," said Minello. "You," he said, pointing to one of the men assembled at the mansion, "Get out to the front gate and secure the area. I'll go in and check on Ricci. The rest of you get the dogs, and search around the property," commanded Minello.

Several moments later, Minello entered the home. There was an armed guard outside of Ricci's study. Minello shot him twice in the head, and moved the body away from the doorway. He entered the den and saw Don Ricci relaxing in a recliner, reading a book. "Dominic, why are the floods off?" he asked, trying to act genuinely concerned.

Without looking up Ricci said, "Marie says she can't sleep when those lights are on."

"I'm really sorry Dominic, but they should always be on at night."

"Well, if you think they need to be on, turn them back on. Marie can learn to live with them."

"I guess so," said Minello. "Dominic, I want you to understand that I am doing this for the Partnership," he added, as he pointed the pistol at Ricci's head and pulled the trigger. The first bullet hit Ricci in the back of his head. The second entered through his right ear. Ricci turned and looked at Minello, just before the first bullet struck its intended target. He saw Minello holding the gun, just prior to its discharge. Ricci tried to say something but slumped in his chair almost immediately after he had been shot. Minello wondered if the surprised look on Ricci's face would be permanently etched into his memory of the Don.

Satisfied that he had stealthily eliminated Ricci, and his

body guard, he removed the silencer from his gun and put it back in his coat pocket. Minello walked back to the front door and went outside. One of the guards was standing watch there, with a shotgun slung over his shoulder and a pistol in his hand. "Is the Don alright?" asked the big burly mobster.

"Unfortunately not, I was too late," Minello said sadly. "The Don and his body guard are dead. They were both shot in the head. It probably happened so fast they didn't know what hit them. Have the men continue to search the premises, but I imagine the killer is long gone by now. I'm going back inside to call the authorities and report the crime," said Minello, obviously shaken.

"I'll tell the guys Paul. Do you want me to get rid of the weapons once we've completed our search?"

"No, you are all licensed to carry firearms. Besides, you were guarding the family. The authorities will understand."

"I'm really sorry about the Don, but honestly we never heard a peep from inside the house," he said, apologetically.

"I know. The guy is a professional killer, and he is very dangerous, resourceful, and cunning. We probably never had much of a chance against him," said Minello resolutely, trying to appear more shaken and distraught the longer he spoke. The guard noticed a couple of tears running down Minello's cheeks, as he turned and reentered the home. Once inside, Minello quickly grabbed a telephone and made a phone call. De Luca answered and listened as Minello talked. "I took care of business a little while ago," said Minello. "Tell the captains about the Don. We'll need to meet at the surplus store tomorrow afternoon and get organized. I'm about ready to call the police. The news account will be in the papers by tomorrow morning. You can tell the Captains it was probably the hit man who killed the Don. I'll see you tomorrow."

"Thanks," Corrado said. "I know it was hard on you, but it had to be done. Deep down, I think our men will be grateful that the old man is gone. I'm going to propose to the Captains tonight that we make you the next Don," promised De Luca.

"Yeah, I know. Thanks. This had to be done for the benefit of the Partnership," said Minello, before he hung up the phone.

As Minello pondered what he was going to tell the authorities, he thought about his actions. These things have to happen every once in a while, he thought, feeling somewhat remorseful now. Over the last few years, the Don had been acting more like an emperor than a Boss. I always liked the Don, as a father figure, but he needed to go. His demise was not personal, it was just business. Our businesses have been suffering under his leadership over the past few years. And the Don has been unwilling to share as much of the profits with the Family as he should have. Don Ricci had always been greedy, but not to this extent. Secretly I've been concerned he might be going senile. In the end, I knew it was the right thing to do for the Partnership, he assured himself.

Ten minutes later, Minello picked up the phone and informed the authorities. Within half an hour, the estate was crawling with cops.

* * *

Meanwhile, Bartlett was ordering a ham and cheese sandwich with a coke, at a drive-in restaurant near the outskirts of Lake Orion. He wanted to wait until after dark before proceeding to Ricci's estate. There were a couple knives, and two 9 mm handguns, with custom made silencers, in his duffle bag. He wore dark clothing, and had night vision goggles and plenty of extra clips. It was ten-thirty, and he was preparing himself to kill Ricci and anyone else who would get in his way.

About thirty minutes earlier, he had seen several police and emergency vehicles, speeding out of town. He wondered where they were going and what emergency they were responding to.

Bartlett paid the car hop, backed out of the parking space, and slowly drove towards the Ricci estate. He planned to park the pickup in an obscure spot and wait in the woods for a while, before breaking into the home.

It was unusually chilly for a late summer evening and, as he drove, he thought about how many times he had done a contract killing before. This time was different though, because he was on a mission to kill for revenge. He knew killing Ricci would be one of the most dangerous and important hits of his life. Bartlett was confident in his abilities, but he knew there were plenty of armed men there waiting to shoot him.

Ten minutes outside of Lake Orion, Bartlett turned onto Ricci's road and headed north. About half a mile down he could see a lone police cruiser, with his flashing lights on, stopped at the intersection. He thought the cop might have stopped someone speeding. As he approached, he could see the officer was not there because someone was speeding, but instead was diverting traffic.

Bartlett debated whether to turn around, but he decided to proceed and see what was going on. He rolled down his window as he approached the intersection. The cop came over to his vehicle and said, "I'm sorry but you'll have to go either right or left. I can't let you go straight."

"What's going on?" Bartlett inquired.

"I'm not sure but supposedly there is a major crime scene three-quarters of a mile from here. The state police asked us not to let anyone pass. Do you live down that way?" the officer inquired.

"No, but to tell you the truth, I've gotten myself lost."

"Where are you headed sir?" asked the officer, politely.

"Lake Orion. I'm supposed to meet some friends there and go fishing on their boat tomorrow," said Bartlett, nonchalantly.

"Well, you are headed north and you need to turn around and go south. You'll be in Lake Orion in about ten minutes."

"Thanks officer for your help," Bartlett said, as he turned the pickup around and headed back towards Lake Orion.

"You're welcome," said the officer. "Glad to help."

I wonder what the hell was really going on, he thought. Ricci's estate is the only property on that stretch of road. I guess I'll go back to Lake Orion, find a room for the night, and look into things tomorrow morning.

* * *

Early Wednesday morning, Bartlett picked up a copy of the Detroit Free Press and was shocked to read that Ricci and two of his body guards had been shot and killed last evening, at his Lake Orion estate. According to the newspaper account, the suspect was an anonymous hit man, who had been threatening the Ricci family. *Evidently, they are blaming the murders on me, he thought.*

In truth, Bartlett was elated the job had been done for him. Although, he would have liked to have seen the look on Ricci's face when he shot and killed him.

Bartlett assumed it was an inside job, and the newspaper story hinted that the Don's underboss, Paul Minello, might have orchestrated a move against Ricci. However, the family attorney assured the authorities that was not the case. He stated that several of the guards, who were at the estate, proclaimed Minello was innocent of the charge. Nevertheless, an anonymous police informant had speculated that Minello might be the Partnership's next Boss.

Realizing there was no reason to continue his stay in Lake Orion; Bartlett quickly packed his bag and drove out of town. It took him about thirty minutes before he abandoned the pickup and retrieved his rental car. It had been a stressful two days, and Bartlett was glad to be back on the Interstate, returning to Chicago.

Chapter 24

Late Friday afternoon, Bartlett returned to St. Croix. His activities in Detroit had been neither totally rewarding nor disappointing. He would have preferred to have killed Ricci himself but he knew that plans do not always work out as intended. Nevertheless, Cavallaro and Ricci were now dead, and his revenge had been secured. In fact, even though the desired results had been achieved, Bartlett would have preferred Moira had never died and that retribution for her killing would not have been necessary. However, he knew that was not his reality. She was dead and those directly responsible for her demise were now dead too.

Bartlett thought it was time to begin moving on with his life, unfortunately, the loving memories of Moira were still haunting him. He had never been happier than the time he was with Moira, and he continued to miss her. The sexual trysts he had been having with Sandra were wonderful but without real meaning. Those encounters were only about sex and they both understood and appreciated the benefits of having an untangled relationship.

However, his feelings for Rosa were different. Every time they made love, he felt magnificent. Nevertheless, sometimes during intercourse, he would become confused about whether he had been having sex with Rosa or Moira. As time passed, he started to hallucinate and would briefly imagine seeing Moira's image, despite the fact he was with Rosa. Bartlett knew it was not normal to be experiencing those kinds of emotional and psychological disorders. He considered going back to the clinic for help but chose not to. With an almost full bottle of Prozac in his medicine cabinet, Bartlett hoped the drug would be helpful when he decided to begin taking it again. However, the doctor at the clinic had told him that if things ever worsened, which they had, he should consider making an appointment to see a psychiatrist. Bartlett had no intention, or interest, in ever allowing a psychiatrist, or any other doctor, to analyze his mind, or his thoughts.

He was resigned that what he had to do to Moira's body in Evanston, was necessary for his own protection. Bartlett thought it was perfectly understandable that guilt, confusion, and the emotional and psychological problems that he continued to encounter remained, and would take a while longer to subdue. He wanted to feel good again and be free to pursue his sexuality with Rosa, Sandra, or any other woman of his choosing, but he imagined it was going to be quite an adjustment. Bartlett wondered how long it might take to rid himself of these problems and maybe try to establish a loving and meaningful relationship with Rosa.

He was thankful that Rosa was extremely happy to have him home. When Bartlett entered the store and saw her standing behind the counter, as their eyes met, she hurriedly greeted him with a kiss and a tender hug. "Welcome home. I've missed you," she said. He knew she was sincere when he saw tears of joy form in her eyes.

Her emotion moved him and he witnessed once again her attachment to him. "It's good to be home," he said, as he kissed and hugged her in return.

Rosa felt herself becoming aroused as she continued to embrace him and tenderly kiss his lips. "I hope you are ready for tonight. I'm really horny," she whispered, softly in his ear.

"Really," he said, with a smile, feeling very fortunate, appreciated, and loved.

"Wait and see. I thought we'd get a quick dinner in town, go home, and get into bed," she said, as she playfully squeezed his buttocks and pressed herself more firmly against him.

"Sounds wonderful," Bartlett said, as he thought about her almost insatiable sexual appetite.

"I can hardly wait until we make love," she said.

"Me too," he said, enthusiastically. "I'll call The Salty Pirate and see if I can get a table for us in an hour.

When they arrived at the restaurant, the maître d' quickly escorted them to Bartlett's favorite table, out on the patio. "Glad to see you again, Mr. Bartlett. Can I bring you a martini?" asked the waiter.

"Yes and bring the lady a Pina Colada please."

"Right away Mr. Bartlett."

After gulping down two dry martinis, Bartlett gazed into Rosa's eyes and asked, "What would you say if I told you I thought we should start living together after my house sells?"

"Oh my God Jim!" Rosa exclaimed, very emotionally. "Are you sure?"

"Yes, I've been thinking about it for a while and I'm ready. I wanted to wait for the right opportunity to ask you," he said. "Would that make you happy?"

"Yes, very happy. You certainly have a way of making me feel special," she said, as she leaned over and gave him a romantic kiss.

"I'm glad I do," he said, smiling at her.

"But … there is something I don't quite understand. Why would you want to sell your house, if we're going to be moving in together? Why can't we just stay there?"

"Well, I need to sell the property to generate some additional funds for my business venture in Miami. I thought we could rent a nice, affordable place, not too far from the shop, instead of trying to buy a less expensive home in Christiansted. Anyway, I thought you would want to be closer to work, particularly when I'm going to be gone more frequently. And, I actually thought you'd want to live in a place that we could consider just ours, instead of living in the same home I've shared with another woman."

"Sure, I would like to live closer, and it would be very nice to have our own place," she said, "But, I never imagined you would need to sell the house if we got together."

After her remarks, Bartlett realized she was troubled and uncomfortable with his plan. He decided to speak rather frankly to her. "I think we need to discuss this matter later," he said, rather coolly. "I'd like to enjoy a good meal and have a pleasant evening with you. However, I'm concerned if we continue having this discussion, our potentially nice evening might be ruined."

"That's fine," she said, trying to assure Bartlett that there was nothing that problematic with his plan. "We can talk about it later if you want," she said. However, Rosa was aware, the only way to get Bartlett to change his mind about anything would be if she could use her carefully crafted, feminine skills on him. She thought Bartlett was stubborn, like most men, who would never change their minds once a decision had been made. But, she was hopeful that if she were allowed to tactfully present her point of view, and reason with him, she would have a better chance to convince him not to sell the house.

After dinner, they hurried home and immediately began an evening of love-making that continued well past midnight.

To Rosa's surprise, the following morning Bartlett arose early and drove into work. He was very anxious to begin implementing his future plans. Shortly after eight o'clock, he called a local realtor and put the property on the market. At the realtor's suggestion, Bartlett decided to offer his home as a private listing. As the realtor explained, the arrangement would allow the property to be shown by appointment only, without any yard signage to attract unwanted attention.

Bartlett surmised Rosa would want to discuss the matter again, because of her unenthusiastic reaction to his plan to sell the house. He also knew how persuasive a woman could be, in order to get her way. Regardless, he knew the home had to be sold for his protection. His overall strategy was to try to eliminate any past, or future, traces of his existence on the island. Bartlett thought getting rid of the home and selling the business to Rosa would accomplish his objectives, allowing him to occasionally stay there and still remain anonymous.

Unbeknownst to Rosa, Bartlett planned to have her be the lessee for the real estate he planned to rent near Christiansted. There were other things he did not plan to reveal to her, including the existence of the leased property in the Cayman Islands, and his new relationship with Sandra White.

Just before noon, Bartlett called Sandra to update her on his timetable for relocating to the Cayman's. She was pleased to hear from him and said she could hardly wait to see him again. Bartlett reassured her that as soon as the property on the Mainland sold, he would be moving. Sandra suggested he make a special trip to the Cayman's, and fairly soon, to begin setting up his new residence and to familiarize himself with the island. Bartlett agreed, and during their conversation she intimated, as a further incentive to get him to come there, that she could hardly wait to get him back into her bedroom.

Bartlett told her that he would plan a return trip for the following weekend and that he could hardly wait to see her too.

* * *

Just before closing the store on Saturday afternoon, Bartlett walked into the shop and casually said to Rosa, "Honey, after you lock the front door please come back to the office."

"Alright," she said. "What's up?"

"Nothing significant, but I want to keep you informed of my plans," said Bartlett, innocently.

"Sure, just give me a couple of minutes."

Several minutes later, Rosa appeared at his office door. Bartlett looked up when he saw her standing in the doorway and said, "My partner in Miami called today. He wants me to come back for a few days to finalize some more arrangements. I know I just got back from Miami, but I need to go there again. I'm really sorry."

"Oh my God," said Rosa, sounding disappointed and perplexed. "You just got back."

"I'm not planning on leaving until next weekend," Bartlett stated. "We'll be together until next Friday. I'm sorry but these things take time. If I didn't have to worry about the shop, I'd take you with me."

Rosa hesitated briefly, thought about her reaction and said, "I'm sorry about being so emotional. I know you have to go, but I'm just a bit frustrated and disheartened. I'll try to be more understanding next time. Please forgive me," she said.

"Don't worry about it honey. I'll only be gone for a couple of days and then I'll be back here for a month or more."

"I was hopeful that you would be able to handle your business dealings in Miami somewhat differently."

"Things will get better," Bartlett assured her. "You'll see."

"I hope they will," she said, with a sigh.

In an attempt to change the subject, Bartlett responded, "I thought we'd stop by the fishing pier before we go home. My buddy said they expect today's catch will be Grouper, your favorite fish. Let's pick up several filets and have fish and chips tonight for dinner."

"I'd love it," she said. "I'll make the citrus sauce that you like while you're firing up the grill."

"Great," said Bartlett.

"After dinner, can we go shopping at the Mall? I need a few more blouses, and the stores are having a big pre-fall sale."

"Sure, whatever you want to do honey," said Bartlett, satisfied Rosa had temporarily forgotten about his travel plans.

Bartlett wondered if he should have introduced the bogus trip to Miami at a more opportune time. Maybe I should have brought it up tomorrow morning, after we had made love. I do not want Rosa to think that there might be another reason for the trip. I don't imagine she would ever suspect that I'm sexually involved with another woman. However, there is no reason for her to know about the new residence in the Cayman's or the fact that I created a bogus business in Miami either.

He had no desire to intentionally hurt Rosa. She had been loyal and he was beginning to have stronger feelings for her. He thought about his overall plan and remembered an earlier discussion that he had with his attorney, concerning who his beneficiary would be, now that Moira was deceased. The lawyer had suggested that he name Rosa as his beneficiary. After all, she would be the surviving business partner in the Ursula Shop upon his death. Besides, he had no living relatives left to leave his assets too. Rosa was really the only reasonable choice. He knew she would be floored, if she ever found out he had made her his heir. She would be shocked to know how much she might someday inherit.

After Moira's death, Bartlett had tentatively decided to continue in business as a paid assassin, at least for a while, or until he decided to retire once again.

Bartlett's purpose for creating the Miami business was to separate himself, his relocation to the Cayman's, and his on-going affair with Sandra, from Rosa. Also, he wanted to allow himself the ability to travel stateside, where he planned to continue conducting his anonymous business. He did not think his temporary absence from work would be a problem. If it had, Bartlett planned to say he had been very ill and had taken some time off to recuperate. After all, he had never announced his intention to retire, or his brief unauthorized retirement, to his contacts in the Chicago mob.

* * *

A week later, after Bartlett had arrived in the Cayman's, he called Anthony Pataldo, the Underboss of the Chicago mob. Pataldo was not surprised to hear from him, since he routinely checked in for referrals. "How are things in the Windy City Mr. Pataldo?" asked Bartlett. "This is John Moore calling."

"Yeah, I know. As usual, it's hotter than hell here," Pataldo said. "What's up Moore?"

"Not much, same old stuff," Bartlett said, innocently. "I was wondering if you had any referrals for me? Also, I changed my contact number again."

"Give it to me, I'll jot it down. Hey, where've you been lately?" Pataldo asked, inquisitively.

"Oh, I've been traveling a little, taking short vacations. I'm trying to get over a brief illness. Why, what's up?" Bartlett responded, innocently.

"I don't have any referrals but I did have an inquiry. Did you do some work for a friend of ours in Detroit recently?" Pataldo asked.

"Yes, why do you ask?" inquired Bartlett, cautiously.

"Their Underboss called me and he said they had been trying to get in touch with you."

"They had my old number."

"He said you wouldn't return his call. Is that right?" asked Pataldo.

"There were some complications."

"What kind?"

"While I was on assignment for them they had planned to double-cross and kill me after I finished their job. A month and a half later, two of their men unexpectedly showed up at my girlfriend's house in Chicago, looking for me."

"How did that go?"

"Not well at all but I handled it. Unfortunately, she got in their way," Bartlett said, reluctantly.

"Why did they try to double-cross you?" asked Pataldo.

"Trying to get back at me for not completing the contract, I guess. That's why they called you too, I suppose."

"Sorry to hear about your girlfriend. Anything I can do?"

"Thanks, but it's too late," said Bartlett, sounding

melancholy. "Shit happens and there is nothing to do but forget about it, and try to move on."

"That's right John, it's best to just forget about it and move on."

Pataldo wondered if Moore had really forgotten about it and moved on. If I was him and somebody killed my girlfriend or spouse, it would be almost impossible for me not to want to seek revenge. After all, Moore is very capable and resourceful when it comes to getting retribution. It's what he does for a living.

"I suppose you're right. Anyway, did you see the story in the Tribune the other day about them? The newspaper speculated that it was an inside job, but I don't know," said Moore.

"Yeah, I don't know either," said Pataldo. They say the new Boss is not old-school, like their former Boss had been."

"Interesting," said Bartlett. "I hear he's already having some major problems. The authorities received some damaging documents about their Family's businesses. Word on the street is their former attorney might have ratted them out, right after he mysteriously disappeared."

"All I know is something happened to the Don. You weren't involved in any of that bullshit, were you Moore?"

"You've got to be kidding me," said Bartlett, with a hint of concern. "Hell no, the guy was a Boss. I didn't have anything to do with it. I'm not crazy."

"Okay, I was just checking," said Pataldo.

"No problem. Everything okay then?" asked Bartlett.

"Yeah, under the circumstances, everything's okay," said Pataldo. "I'm glad we don't have their problems," said the mobster. "Keep in touch Moore."

"Will do," said Bartlett, as he quickly hung up the phone.

Chapter 25

A week later, on Thursday afternoon, Bartlett left St. Croix for the Cayman Islands. Previously he had told Rosa he was going to be in Miami on business. When he arrived at the Owen Roberts International Airport in George Town, Sandra was waiting to greet him in her BMW, outside the airport terminal. Thus began a remarkable two-day visit to Grand Cayman.

Originally they had planned to work on his residence, but those plans were temporarily put on hold. Instead, he spent the days touring with Sandra, familiarizing him with the island, and nights pleasuring her in the bedroom. Even though he was having a wonderful time with her, late Saturday morning Bartlett began packing for home. He had promised Rosa he would be back in St. Croix no later than Sunday afternoon, and he had no intention of disappointing her.

Unbeknownst to Bartlett, while he showered, Sandra placed an envelope containing a Polaroid, and a note, in a small, obscure, zippered cloth side compartment in his suitcase. She hoped that its contents would surprise and please him.

All of his return flights into St. Croix, whether from the Cayman Islands or the Mainland, were purposely routed through San Juan International Airport. Whenever Bartlett arrived back at the St. Croix airport, he always remembered to remove the small tags attached to his suitcase by the airlines, and dispose of his remaining boarding passes, prior to returning home.

Late Saturday evening, Bartlett was on an American Airlines flight from San Juan back to St Croix, scheduled to arrive at ten-thirty. He wanted to surprise Rosa by coming home earlier than expected. It was late when Bartlett finally pulled into his driveway. A light was on in the living room when he entered the house. "I'm home honey," he yelled, after laying down his suitcase.

Almost immediately, Rosa appeared from the bedroom and greeted him with a warm smile, a hug, and a kiss. "How did it go in Miami?" she asked.

"Fine. I got a lot done, and I don't think I'll need to go back for at least a month."

"That sounds great," she said. "Are you hungry?"

"No, I ate in Miami."

"Oh, alright," she said. "If you hand me your suitcase I'll put your clean clothes away and wash the dirty clothes tomorrow morning."

"That's nice but not necessary," Bartlett said, trying to seem considerate. "I can do it tomorrow," he said, preferring to do it himself.

"Are you sure?" Rosa responded.

"Yeah, it's been a long day and I'm tired. If you don't mind, I'd rather we just go to bed."

"Sure, I can take care of it tomorrow," she said, as she switched off the living room light and followed him into the bedroom.

Shortly after kissing her goodnight, Bartlett fell asleep. However, Rosa wasn't really tired, so she continued reading the romance novel she had bought in the pharmacy. She wondered why his business trip had been so tiring for him. Normally she would expect him to want sex upon his return, but she decided not to worry about it. A half-hour later she closed her book and laid it on the night stand, switched off the table lamp, and quickly went to sleep.

At eight o'clock the following morning, they awoke, went to the bathroom, and quickly climbed back into bed. A few minutes later, Bartlett began to passionately kiss and caress her body. Their love making continued for almost an hour, until they were satisfied, and had drifted off to sleep.

Rosa awoke at eleven o'clock. Bartlett was still in bed, sleeping, when she got up. She gathered his dirty laundry and put it into the washing machine, unpacked his suitcase, and emptied his Dopp kit. She noticed several Trojan condoms in the clear plastic hanging bag, inside the kit, and wondered why they were there. *Maybe he had forgotten they were there, she thought, before she put them back in the opened box in the cabinet drawer.*

Around eleven-thirty, Bartlett awoke and strolled into the kitchen. He was pleasantly surprised to see Rosa making a late breakfast for them. When he entered the room, he could hear the churning of the washing machine. "Are you washing my clothes?" he asked. "Thanks, but you know I could have done it myself."

"I know you're a very self-sufficient man, but I didn't think you'd mind if I helped you out," she said smiling.

Bartlett reluctantly agreed. "Thanks," he said. A few minutes later, after he read the newspaper's local weather, he said, "It's going to be a beautiful day, with very calm seas. Want to rent a boat and go to Buck Island this afternoon?" he asked.

"Sure, we don't have anything better to do," she said. "Sounds like fun. We can take some meat, cheese, fruit, and a few cold drinks and have a late lunch too. How soon do you want to go?"

"How about right now?" said Bartlett.

"Okay but I'll need fifteen minutes to freshen up and pack," said Rosa, enthusiastically.

Forty-five minutes later, they were on the eastern side of the island, at the marina. Around one-thirty, Bartlett and Rosa were motoring towards the National Park. When they arrived, Bartlett secured the powerboat not far from the shoreline, and they carefully waded toward the sandy beach. Surprisingly there were very few people to share the Park with that day. Rosa easily located a partially shaded area, where she placed their cooler. Meanwhile, Bartlett spread out two large beach towels for them to recline, sun bathe, and relax on.

After lunch, a short nap, and some casual conversation, Bartlett decided it was time to begin weaving several fabricated stories about himself, with her. Going forward, his intention was to cover up his criminal activities and deceive Rosa further, as he had planned to do. He waited several minutes to speak, until after she had commented about what a good idea it was to come to Buck Island that afternoon, after which he blurted out a very serious question to her. "Rosa, can I trust you completely with my life?" he inquired, very bluntly.

Surprised that Bartlett would have to ask such a ridiculous question, Rosa responded with a simple, "Yes, absolutely you can," she said, half disturbed and wondering why he would ask such a question.

"Good," he said, with a relieved look on his face. "I've got something very important to tell you about myself. It probably will shock and surprise you and maybe make you mad."

"What is it?" she asked.

"I've been keeping secrets from you, for a long time. In the beginning, I didn't think I had much of a choice. However, once we became involved in this amazing relationship, I knew I'd have to tell you as much as I'm allowed to say. I trust you, and hope you'll be able to understand why I've kept you in the dark for so long."

"What secrets?" she asked inquisitively.

"Well, here goes," he said, sighing momentarily, before speaking, "I'm a covert agent for the United States Central Intelligence Agency. The real reason I am selling the house is because I need extra money to have two homes, one in St. Croix and the other in Miami. I don't have another business in Florida but I've been permanently assigned to work there by the government."

"Okay, go on," said Rosa, as she continued to listen to him, with a look of amazement on her face.

"Over the last several years I've been directed, by the Federal government, to do highly classified work outside of St. Croix. Now you know what I've really been doing on those business trips off the island."

"What kinds of things do you do?" she asked.

"Believe me, you don't really want to know. All I can tell you is that I have been doing some very important assignments, mostly in and around the Caribbean."

"How long have you been an agent?" asked Rosa, very inquisitively.

"Close to thirty years. I joined the Agency after I got out of the Army. I'm also a Vietnam veteran."

"Gosh Jim, in a thousand years, I would have never guessed you were a government agent" Rosa said, almost in disbelief.

"I'm very good at what I do," he stated, proudly. "I hope this will explain why I've gone ahead and made several decisions that I know you didn't want me to make."

"I guess I'm beginning to understand," she said, almost astounded by what he had just revealed.

"In fairness to you, I've felt very badly about deceiving you, since we're in a very serious relationship. Please understand that you will never be able to tell anyone about me or my activities with the Federal government. You do understand that, don't you?"

Without hesitation, Rosa said "Yes, I understand. I'll never tell anyone about you. I promise," she said, sounding like she was a Government official herself.

"Good," said Bartlett, acting like he was satisfied with her pronouncement.

* * *

Several weeks later, Bartlett was becoming increasingly aware that Rosa sometimes acted oddly around him. More than once, he caught her giving him a cold stare. Bartlett knew that she probably had plenty of questions about his past, but apparently had decided not to bring them up yet.

He was not too concerned about her, but he wondered what was going on in her head. Bartlett thought maybe this was her way of trying to accept him as the person she now knew, the rogue government agent, rather than the person she thought she had known before.

Bartlett figured, eventually, she would get used to being with a person with a dual identity and begin treating him normally again. However, he thought her attitude was somewhat different as well. It didn't surprise him that he could not quite figure her out. After all, she was a very emotionally charged woman, typical for a person of Italian and Puerto Rican descent.

Another couple of weeks passed and Bartlett noticed that the old Rosa, with whom he had established a meaningful relationship, was finally returning. He was relieved, thinking she had finally gotten over what had been troubling her.

He wondered if he had made a mistake by telling her that he had been deceiving her. The lingering question was: Did he think that someday he might need to get rid of her? He hoped not. Bartlett felt assured that nothing needed to be done for the time being.

Nevertheless, he thought it might be helpful to go out of his way and show her how much he really cared and appreciated her. With that purpose in mind, Bartlett decided to ask her to temporarily close the shop and take a mini-vacation with him to another adjacent island.

St. John was the smallest, least populated, but most commercialized, of the three islands comprising the United States Virgin Islands chain. The island offered many beautiful resort destinations, plenty of pristine beaches, and lots of upscale shopping. Bartlett quickly arranged for a romantic weekend get-a-way to St. John, and they spent several days at a luxurious resort, shopping, sightseeing, relaxing, and making love.

Rosa seemed happy, although at times, he thought he

could still recognize a slight coolness in her eyes, even after they had returned home.

As the days passed Rosa was thankful that, under her direction, the shop was making plenty of money, and Bartlett had kept his word and given her total autonomy. Occasionally, when he was in town, he would stop at the shop to visit her during the day. He was impressed by the increased customer counts and sales and the amount of stylish clothing and collectibles that she had on display.

On one of those occasions, when Bartlett was in St. Croix, Rosa stopped at the fish market and bought several Grouper filets for dinner. The butcher assured her that it was the "fresh catch" of the day. However, she questioned their freshness due to a slight odor she noticed during preparation.

Bartlett was happy to be home and for a home-cooked meal. It had been more than two weeks since he completed his last contractual killing in the States. Ever since he had changed his telephone number, it seemed like he would never run out of work. He was very thankful for the jobs and the opportunity to be back in business.

He was glad to be home and to be with Rosa. He missed seeing Sandra White too, though he had quite a different relationship with her. Balancing two relationships at once was becoming quite a challenge and quite a time commitment.

After eating a delicious meal and enjoying the usual cup of hot tea, he and Rosa shared a marvelous sunset, some casual conversation, and a few drinks before bedtime. Several hours later, after they had been in bed a while, Bartlett awoke with a stomach ache. He thought it might be food poisoning, but began to feel better after several trips to the bathroom.

The following morning Rosa came into the bedroom with a large cup of hot tea, upon learning Bartlett's stomach was still bothering him. "I put an old family recipe in your tea this morning," she said. "My grandmother used to take it every time she had a stomach ache."

"Thanks. I hope it does the trick. My stomach still doesn't feel that well," he said. "See you tonight."

"It always worked for my grandmother," stated Rosa, as she bent down and gave him an overly affectionate goodbye kiss. "See you tonight," she said, as she smiled and quickly walked through the bedroom door into the living room.

Rosa arrived at the shop and opened for business promptly at eight a.m. Business had been hectic most of the day, and Rosa had not checked on his condition. Promptly at five o'clock, she locked the front door of the Ursula Shop and headed home. The eastern bus route was perfect for her, because it passed just a block away from the new house.

Together, they had selected a stylish, 1,200 square foot, single bedroom condo, because of its location to the shop and because it had been newly updated within the past six months. It only took them a short time to move in. The home seemed adequate and roomy after Rosa had rearranged some of the furniture. Fortunately Bartlett had been able to sell his hillside property for a hefty profit, giving Rosa a sizeable budget for additional furniture purchases.

Rosa only had to wait a few minutes before her bus arrived. She happily climbed aboard and selected a seat near the front. As people boarded and departed the bus, Rosa made a habit of greeting them politely, when she saw a familiar face. At her normal stop, she got off and walked home.

The house was quiet when she entered the kitchen through the back door. She laid down her bag and proceeded to the sink, pouring herself a tall glass of water. "I'm home," she yelled into the living room. Hearing no response, she slowly walked into the living room and approached the bedroom door. When she peered through the doorway, she saw that Bartlett was still in bed. As she approached him, Rosa could see that something was terribly wrong -- Bartlett was not breathing. She touched his face and felt his skin. He was cold as ice. Rosa knew he was dead.

Frantically she grabbed the phone and quickly called for an ambulance. Ten minutes later, the ambulance arrived along with the police. The EMT's examined his body and quickly notified the island coroner, who came a short time later and pronounced Bartlett officially dead.

Thirty minutes later, a policeman, familiar to Rosa and the island coroner, came over to talk with her while she sat weeping and nervously shaking on the couch. "Ms.

Rodriguez, my name is Dr. Mancini and I think you already know Officer Caulier. We're very sorry about your loss."

Looking up at the men, she responded, "Yes, hello officers. Thank you," she said, as she wiped the tears from her face with a Kleenex.

"Do you mind if I ask you some questions?" Dr. Mancini inquired.

"No, what do you want to know?" she said.

"What was your relationship to the deceased?"

"He was my boyfriend and my business partner," Rosa said.

"Had Mr. Bartlett been ill lately?"

"Well, he was having problems with his stomach last evening. Frankly, I think he had a reaction of some kind to the fish we had for dinner."

"I see," said Dr. Mancini. "Were there any other things that might have been wrong with him?"

"As far as I know he was really healthy, but lately he had been experiencing some emotional and psychological problems," Rosa stated.

"What kind of problems?" asked the doctor.

"Well, we had been having some troubles for a couple of weeks, concerning our relationship," she said, candidly. "However, those problems seemed to be settled," she interjected.

"Okay. Were there any other problems that you were aware of?" he asked, inquisitively.

"For as long as I've known him, Jim has always had trouble sleeping, and lately he's been plagued with nightmares. Recently, he told me he had hallucinated about some event that had occurred during the war."

"When was he in the military?" asked Mancini.

"About thirty years ago, I guess. He told me he was an Army combat soldier and had fought in the Vietnam War."

"Was he being treated by a doctor for those problems?"

"I guess so, but he never made a big deal about it. Six weeks ago he went to see a doctor at the out-patient clinic, next to the St. Croix Hospital. He told me the doctor had given him a prescription."

"What kind of prescription? Do you know the name of the drug that he had been taking?"

"Sure, it was Prozac. The bottle is in our medicine cabinet, in the bathroom. I can get it for you, if you want to see it," volunteered Rosa.

"That won't be necessary, but thank you. The officers will find it before they're finished."

"Alright," she said, trying to be helpful.

"Ms. Rodriguez, did Jim ever attempt to intentionally hurt himself?" asked Mancini, trying to be as sensitive to her feelings as possible.

"Not that I am aware of but I'm certain Jim would never do anything to hurt himself," she said, obviously objecting to any suggestion that this may have been intentional. "That's not my Jim," she said, as she stared at the doctor and began to cry. "He's always been a very happy person and contented with his life." she said.

Mancini was not surprised to hear how happy she had thought her deceased boyfriend might have been with his life. And, he also witnessed her very sorrowful and doubtful reaction, to his insinuation that it may have been suicide. "We can stop here for now," he said, realizing that he wanted to try to help her cope with the tragedy. "I don't have any more questions for you right now but where can I get in touch with you later?" he asked.

"I'll be here. This is my home too," said Rosa. "I'm going to take some time off and temporarily close the business. I've got a lot of decisions to make prior to the funeral," she said, as she began to cry again.

"Thanks for your time and patience with me," Mancini stated. "If there is anything I can do to help you, please let me know," he said, as her gently held her hand for several moments, attempting to console her.

Mancini arose from the couch and walked to the other side of the room. He motioned for Caulier to join him there. When Caulier arrived, Mancini quietly said to him, "After looking over the scene, my initial opinion is there was no foul play here. It's a typical suicide, but first, I'm going to run some tests to determine the cause of death."

"I'd be very surprised, if there was any foul play," said Caulier. "Ms. Rodriguez has an outstanding reputation in the community."

"Did your men find a suicide note in the room?" asked Mancini.

"No, there was nothing there. Besides, these ex-service guys don't always leave a note when they kill themselves," stated Caulier.

"I know. I was just curious," said Mancini.

"However, we did find a half-empty, opened bottle of Prozac, on the bathroom counter and a large coffee cup. It looks and smells like he might have been drinking tea."

"Have your men bag the cup and the Prozac. They can put it on the front seat of my van. I'll take a look at them back at the lab," instructed Mancini.

"Will do," said Caulier.

"I think we can wrap things up here," said Mancini. "I've seen enough. Oh, before you leave, would you have your men assist me in getting the body loaded and secured in my van? It should only take a couple of minutes," said Mancini.

"Sure, glad to help."

Several minutes later, Rosa saw a large, black plastic, elongated bag, with Bartlett's body inside, being secured on top of the coroner's gurney. She watched as the police officers slowly began moving his corpse through the house and out into the yard. The realization that Bartlett had died was sinking in. She began to cry uncontrollably, as she watched them carefully lift and secure the gurney inside the white medical van.

Chapter 26

It was nine-fifteen that evening, when Dr. Mancini finally returned to the morgue with Bartlett's body. He opened the overhead door and parked the van inside the building. His lab assistant was still there, waiting for him to return. It took Mancini and his assistant fifteen minutes to remove the gurney from the van, take it into the laboratory, and put the corpse into a refrigerated compartment.

"Thanks for waiting around to help," Mancini said to his assistant.

"Frankly, I didn't think I had much of a choice doctor," said the assistant. "We never know when these things are going to occur, do we? Was it a suicide?"

"Yes, I think so but I need to check several things, before I can make it official. I might even have to do an autopsy. You can go home for now. I'll see you in the morning."

* * *

Rosa awoke at five o'clock the following morning. Not surprisingly, she had not been able to get very much sleep. Bartlett's death was a traumatic event and she was not prepared to make any funeral arrangements yet. To keep the funeral costs to a minimum, she thought about cremation and a simple graveside service, where only her closest friends would attend. After all, she knew Bartlett had purposely tried not to acquire friends or many casual acquaintances in his life.

Rosa wondered what life without Bartlett would be like. Emotionally, she was spent. She had already cried buckets of tears and had practically made herself physically sick. Rosa knew she would miss him tremendously. She thought it would be hard to love another man, even if he had most of Bartlett's characteristics. She wondered whether she would be able to make it on her own, with only the shop's profits and limited funds in the checking account.

She thought about when she had arranged for her late husband's burial service, several years before. Rosa had been pleased with the services provided by the Johnson-Price Mortuary Chapel, so she decided to give them a call. The funeral director was glad to hear from her again but sadden that their services were needed so suddenly and unexpectedly, once again. Rosa and the funeral director discussed various funeral options and he agreed to help her with financing options. Also, he assured her that he would contact the Coroner and find out when Bartlett's body would be available for burial.

Rosa wondered whether she should notify the Central Intelligence Agency but decided it would not be a good idea to get involved. After all, Bartlett had sworn her to secrecy concerning those matters.

* * *

The previous day had been very tedious and time consuming for Dr. Mancini. Normally, he looked forward to drinking many glasses of rum and coke, and watching Jay Leno on The Tonight Show before going to bed. Mancini was semi-retired and a functioning alcoholic, perfect for a municipality with a limited budget, when it came time to employing a part-time Coroner. The doctor had the skills to be competent but not the ambition to be thorough. Generally, his cases involved the deaths of criminals or victims of drug related crimes. Occasionally, there would be an accidental death, a crime of passion, or even a suicide to work on. Mancini never had to complain about being overworked. Questionable deaths were few and far between on the island. Mancini made it a practice to cut corners on most of his investigations.

Mancini arrived at the morgue at quarter past ten. He had given himself permission to sleep-in, due to working later than usual the night before. After several cups of coffee, Mancini was ready to go to work.

He, and his assistant, began by examining the bottle of Prozac, looking at the prescription date, counting the number of pills that remained, and trying to determine how many tablets Bartlett may have consumed.

They analyzed the residue inside the cup and determined the liquid had been tea. There was no trace of Prozac, or anything else other than tea, in the residue. Mancini concluded that if a large overdose of Prozac was the cause of the decedent's death, it was not a result of someone intentionally putting the drug into his drink.

After completing a routine urine analysis, they discovered a large concentration of Prozac, far exceeding any normal limit that would have ever been prescribed, still in Bartlett's system. Deciding to look further, he made a five inch incision into Bartlett's stomach and noted the absence of any remaining whole Prozac tablets, in his gut. He conducted an unofficial laboratory test, using only hot tea and some Prozac tablets, immersed for fifteen minutes, in a similar cup. The results showed that half of the tablets had not been totally dissolved. However, he concluded that the hot tea along with the corrosive acids in a normal stomach might have been enough to completely dissolve the pills.

Further, they tested Bartlett's body for the presence of any excess serotonin caused by the Prozac in his system. Mancini was not surprised when the test revealed that Bartlett had twenty times the normal amount of the substance in his brain. When he researched the effects of a high concentration of serotonin in a human brain, the doctor concluded that the results were very disturbing. He understood that, within minutes, an excessive amount of serotonin in the brain can produce high blood pressure, hyperthermia, high body temperature, and an increased heart rate, which can lead to shock. Once the onset of shock occurs, the oxygen-rich blood supply to the brain is reduced, and without its almost immediate restoration, within four to five minutes, those brain cells will become damaged causing a stroke and likely death.

Mancini had seen suicides involving overdoses of drugs before but he knew this was the first time he had seen any death associated with Prozac. He was convinced Bartlett had killed himself but surprised that he had used drugs to do it. Normally, he knew that men kill themselves more violently than women. Typically they end their lives with guns but women prefer to use less violent methods.

At four in the afternoon, Mancini concluded his investigation and began filling out the United States Virgin Islands official death certificate form, indicating that Bartlett had died as a result of suicide. He listed the cause of death as a stroke. The time of death was listed between nine and ten a.m., on the previous day, which Mancini had calculated after finishing his initial examination.

Afterwards, Mancini called Officer Caulier to report his findings and notified the Johnson-Price funeral director, that Bartlett's body was ready to be released for burial.

* * *

The following morning, a Johnson-Price representative called Rosa to inform her that they had picked up Bartlett's body at the morgue. The secretary asked Rosa if she had decided on the arrangements yet. She told them to cremate him and make arrangements for a small, grave-side service. She indicated a Catholic priest had been contacted and would be officiating the ceremony.

* * *

Three days later, Rosa put Bartlett to rest in the same cemetery where she had buried her former husband. As expected, the funeral service was lightly attended. And, expectedly, she was the sole person sitting in front of the casket, in lieu of the family. At the conclusion of the ceremony, and as the casket was being lowered into the vault, Rosa became emotionally distraught again and slowly began to weep. Afterwards, she stayed at the grave site until the workman had finished covering up his tomb. When they left, she lowered her head and began to cry again. Bartlett was gone forever. *What am I going to do without him in my life she wondered once again?*

* * *

Two weeks later, Rosa called Henry Culebra, Bartlett's attorney, informing him about Bartlett's tragic death. She scheduled an appointment through Culebra's secretary to discuss the Ursula Shop's business agreement. Promptly, on Friday morning, she flew to San Juan, the capital city of the Commonwealth of Puerto Rico, to meet with the lawyer. His offices were located in an impressive high rise in downtown San Juan.

When she entered the firm's reception area an attractive secretary greeted her and quickly escorted her into Culebra's office. "Mr. Culebra, I'm Rosa Rodriguez, Jim Bartlett's business partner," she said, extending her hand.

"It's very nice to meet you Ms. Rodriguez. Sorry to hear about your loss."

"Thank you," she said. "It's been very hard."

"Quite understandable," he said. "Can I get you something to drink?" asked Culebra.

"No thank you," Rosa responded. "I'd like to get down to business right away. I have an early afternoon flight to catch," she said.

"That's not a problem," said Culebra, pointing to an upholstered chair in front of his desk. "Please have a seat and we will get started."

"Thank you," she said politely, as she laid down her purse and gracefully lowered herself on the chair.

"We have some very important things to talk about," said the lawyer. "Were you aware that Mr. Bartlett named you as his sole beneficiary?" asked Culebra.

"No. What does that mean?" asked Rosa, very inquisitively.

"Ms. Rodriguez, it means that you not only inherit his business interest in the Ursula Shop, but also you will be getting his personal belongings, and most importantly, a large investment account in the Cayman Islands worth, I believe, several million dollars."

"That's not possible, is it?" she said, totally shocked.

"Oh, but it is," he exclaimed. A year ago, I recommended that he consider doing some tax and estate planning. I had him send me copies of his financial investments before ever discussing a proposal for his estate. There is no doubt about it. I was rather surprised too by how much he had accumulated. I never realized how much money an amateur black jack player could win."

"Jim was a gambler?"

"Yes, once he told me he had played in almost every casino in the country over a thirty-year span."

"I had no idea," said Rosa. *I wonder if I will ever really know who Jim Bartlett was, she thought.*

"Funny thing, he never felt the obligation to report his black jack winnings. I guess because it was all in cash. I never questioned him, because someone else did his tax returns.

"That's very interesting. What affect is his death going to have on his taxes now?"

"Probably nothing, that's why people do business in the Cayman's. It's totally confidential and even if there are inquiries by the United States government, they can generally be ignored. That is unless he is a drug dealer or a member of an organized crime family. I'd recommend you keep the investment account as it is and let their people continue to handle everything for you. I'll notify them concerning his death and the change in ownership."

"What else am I supposed to do?" she asked, still in total disbelief.

"I'll help you with all the arrangements. It will probably take me a couple of months or so, to get things in order, before I'll be able to turn everything over to you. Just keep in touch with my secretary," he said. "And, congratulations on your good fortune Ms. Rodriguez. I know you were an excellent and loyal business partner, very committed, and obviously very close to my client."

"Yes, I was all that and more. Thank you so much again, for all your help," said Rosa, obviously continuing to be overwhelmed and shocked by the news. "I'll do exactly as you say."

"It was very nice meeting you Ms. Rodriguez. Good luck and I'll see you again in a few months," he said, as he escorted her to the receptionist's desk.

On the return flight back to St. Croix, Rosa sat almost stoically as she gazed at the clouds outside her window. Her thoughts drifted back to all the things that had happened in her life. She had been totally blown away, when she heard the lawyer say his investment account was worth millions, and that it was soon going to be hers.

Tears of joy and sorrow appeared when she thought about Bartlett again, and what they had done to, and for, each other. She folded her hands over her face, leaned forward in the seat, and began to quietly weep. Her thoughts went to how she was going to have to conceal another secret about her life.

Prior to leaving for the airport, to catch the morning flight to San Juan, Rosa thought about how many times she had examined the contents in the large manila envelope that she had hidden inside her dresser drawer.

The envelope contained personal documents that she had looked at, read, and thought about on numerous occasions. Inside there was a copy of her business agreement with Bartlett, several fictitious named passports with his photo, and drivers licenses from various states with fictitious names, a birth certificate for John Bartkowski, Bartlett's death certificate, a 3X5 index card with the name and phone number for an Anthony Pataldo in Chicago, a copy of a lease agreement he had recently signed for a property in the Cayman Islands, a Cayman Investment firm document with a contact name and phone number, his obviously outdated last will and testament; and also inside was a small lavender scented envelope that held a color Polaroid of a naked, and provocatively posed, pretty blond woman, along with a short note.

Upon seeing the photo and reading the note, Rosa remembered feeling betrayed, heart-broken, stupid, humiliated, and furious. She had accidentally found the small envelope in his suitcase, after she had discovered several condoms in his Dopp kit. Rosa realized the date on the note was the same time that Bartlett had supposedly been in Miami, handling business. The note read: *My*

John W. Gemmer

Darling Jim – Thanks for another wonderful weekend and for the beautiful pearl necklace. Every time I wear it I will always remember our first date. I can hardly wait for your return to my bedroom. Lovingly, Sandra

CPSIA information can be obtained
at www.ICGtesting.com
Printed in the USA
FSOW02n1055011016
25528FS